FAIREST FLESH

BY K.P. KULSKI

Published by Strangehouse Books
an imprint of Rooster Republic Press LLC
www.rooosterrepublicpress.com
roosterrepublicpress@gmail.com

Copyright © by K.P. Kulski 2020
Cover Design by Nicholas Day and Don Noble
Edited by Nicholas Day
Interior Design – Don Noble

ISBN: 978-1-946335-35-7

Find our catalog at
www.roosterrepublicpress.com

FAIREST FLESH

PART I
IN THE WOODS OF HUNGARY

1

The year 1559

Hanga pointed to the rabbit in the snare. "Get it." Most children at this young age still bore some charm that kept parents doting, but Hanga's girl had been a prune from the start. Hanga did not dote on anyone and least of all this ugly child.

The girl lifted the trap, her lumpy face brightening. "Momma, can we keep this one?"

"Bah, you need to learn that's there more important things than furry creatures. There's power and the powerless. What do you think you'll eat for dinner?"

The girl scrunched up her face. "I don't need to eat meat tonight. I'll just eat the greens. I don't want to eat meat ever again." Little Dorottya peered into the cage with a frown, dull eyes turning glassy.

Life's harsh lessons would be worse for this child, looking as she did. She needed skills and toughness. She had grown old enough to learn both.

"Come on, girl. We've got to get back."

The rabbit hunched within the trap, frozen in quiet terror, waiting for the end. It knew, as much as Hanga knew, that life held no comfort, only pain. *Medicine and truth.*

"You can eat the greens," Hanga said when they returned to the tiny cabin. The sun rapidly closed the distance between the

7

dome of the sky and the treetops.

"Really?" Dorottya perked up, hope dawning over her features. "I can keep it? Can I name it?"

"Yes," Hanga said. Best to learn when attached. Medicine was rarely needed in times of calm or with strangers.

She let the girl hold the tiny thing, not much meat on the animal for eating anyhow. They ate greens together and the rabbit relaxed, tricking itself into hoping.

Hope is a trick.

Comfort is a trick.

Asleep, the child curled around her pet, fingers entwined in its fur. Peacefully, both dreamed in the warmth of their new companionship.

Rabbits scream when they are hurt, just like people. When the stone Hanga held smashed the legs of the rabbit, it woke Dorottya, who jumped to her feet and joined in with her own panicked shrieks. She rushed and sobbed and tried to soothe the creature she loved. It bit her in its terror and pain.

Good.

"Now it is time to learn medicine," Hanga said, dropping the reddened stone.

2

The year 1568

Hanga handled the new bud, gently, one among the many in this clearing. The blooms were a lovely sight, both for the delicate snowy cups and the unique medicine that only she knew how to brew. Time to teach the girl, someone to pass it all along to.

Dorottya plodded over, her arms gangly, the rest of her body would catch up but it wouldn't help make the girl any less homely. Hanga felt her lips curl. She no longer tried to disguise her repulsion. Best the girl knew disgust and accepted it. When she grew to womanhood, it would be all anyone would ever see.

Soon the entire clearing would fill with the blooms turning the ground into a blanket of perfumed, snowy white. They would last into the frosts of early winter. Gathered at the right times, the petals eradicated pain or, with enough of a concentration, eradicated life. Hanga showed the bud to Dorottya, carefully opening the petals. In the center, a small pot of red contrasted against the white.

"They only grow here," Hanga said.

Dorottya's eyes widened with interest. She'd become a good pupil, with a natural gift for brewing and fortunetelling.

"Corpse poppies are good for pain," Hanga said. "And good for killing."

"Killing," Dorottya echoed.

"Only when enough is used," Hanga said. "Like most poppies, whoever takes drafts of what you brew, they will want more, so you mustn't use it often, unless of course . . . you want them to want more."

The girl's face turned, furtive.

Hanga dipped a finger into the red center. "This holds the most potency, although the petals can also be used as a sleep agent. A small amount mixed with nightshade produces an inert effect on the body. A person or animal will become unable to use their limbs or move, but can swallow and are awake. However, the tongue will not obey speech. If continually administered thereafter, it will cause eventual death." Hanga said with a scornful smirk, "I'm sure you can imagine uses for such a thing."

"Yes," Dorottya said. A large bruise on the girl's face had just begun to fade. Stupid girl needed to learn how to properly launder linen. A large jutting rock in the stream taught her the lesson well. Since then, their linens had been well washed. Very well, indeed. "I can think of many."

"Good," Hanga said, rising to her feet.

"Mother?"

"What is it?"

The girl kneeled, studied the bloom closely.

"Well? What is it girl?"

Dorottya looked at Hanga. The girl's eyes widened and she gripped at her skirts like a kneading cat. "Who is my father?"

The question shot through Hanga like a blade made of ice. Dark anger followed hotly behind it. She'd lived a lifetime of punishment for that man with this child, his hideous spawn.

"Your father?" Hanga sneered. "Your father was the devil himself." She stalked away and, calling out over her shoulder, she finished, "That is why you look the way you do—sin, girl. Sin made flesh."

3

The year 1573

Dorottya tied a rope around her mother's stiffening ankles and dragged the empty husk to the gravesite. The first light of the deep woods was not the same as light out in the open world. Dawn arrived gray and broke through the canopy as a shadow maker, painting some leaves black, others vibrant green.

Deep graves were difficult to dig in the woods. Tree roots knotted underground and resisted intrusion, so best to dig around each root, making underground caves and tunnels. The deceased rarely rested flat but were forced into unnatural curves, like worms frozen in a moment of movement. If a body could not accommodate the trees, then they were given to flames, cooked and melted so as to keep the wolves at bay. And though the roots were deprived of the entirety of the dead, they still took their due in ashes and oozing fat absorbed eagerly by the dirt. The few who lived in the woods, the outcasts, the forgotten and unwanted, knew the trees ruled everything.

"You aren't going to find happiness out there," mother had often said, motioning to Dorottya's face. "Out there they want beauty. You are many things, but you are not beautiful."

Mother's cough had been the sound of crisp winter leaves, long dead and curled, rattling and scraping in the wind. When Dorottya spooned broth and herbal infusions into the woman's

11

mouth, her tongue laid still, a pale slug bathed in juiced marrow and leaves. As the winter turned long, mother became folds of flesh and jutting bone, her eyes like fixed, dark buttons. She talked no more of beauty.

"Ugly Dorottya," mother had said, "so ugly." She took her last shuddering breath in the early hours of a late-winter morning.

Dorottya held her breath. Putting mother in the ground, to watch the dirt fleck and collapse over her unmoving face, produced a feeling of possibility. Above ground, the trees ate air and sunlight, sprouted leaves, fruit and flowers. But underground, the trees ate the dead, sucked at the damp rot of things that have come and gone. Some said that grave trees gave souls no rest, punishing them to have to twist and bend forever around the shape of suffering.

Ugly. Dorottya imagined her mother's mouth opening and closing over the word, like chewing a nugget of foul meat. *Ugliest I've ever seen.* The memory drained, became vacant, without shape or form, a glob of darkness too terrifying to examine closely.

Now that the roots had their due, a new awareness overtook her, absent of leaves and dirt, whispering an indescribable vastness.

It wouldn't matter if she were ugly.

She could bring beauty, even if she didn't have it.

She could . . .

The trees sighed long, lifting their leaves in disagreement.

IN 1592 . . .

. . . the interrogator asked, "How many girls were killed?"

600.

Perhaps, only 55.

"I can't be sure," she said.

"Why?"

The same reason men stare and want and covet. The same reason beautiful poets look into mirrors long after they've been broken.

———

Once upon a time . . . in the castle above the stream in Sárvár, in the stone cottage, under the water, gurgling and spitting, nearby, in the mirror, locked within the straps of their minds.

There was a beautiful princess.

And she did not live happily ever after.

The trail from the forest turned into a well-used road that leveled with the flatness of the landscape and led to a village that arched up from the ground, bathed in the butter-yellow of late-afternoon sun. Air thickened with the scent of manure. Newly sprouted crops poked through the dirt, small and thin enough to show the soil beneath.

A few notes of music wafted through the air and Dorottya smiled. The melody soon grew boisterous, making her stride longer, eager, her feet nimble, hips swaying. Colorful ribbons tied to posts and garlanding windows waved in greeting, pushing a thrill through her chest. She twirled and laughed.

Free. Truly alive for the first time.

Loud conversation echoed from groups of villagers, slapping their thighs and sloshing wine onto the dirt. Lanterns hung from walls and posts and gave jovial faces half shadows as the sun finally slipped below the horizon. A few danced, their faces ruddy with wine and exertion, girls in pretty laced dresses and red scarves, their beaded necklaces swaying. Dorottya breathed them in, pretending that the arching eyebrows and shapely bodies were hers to wield. Alive with the desire for worship, she cast her flushed lips toward a young man who watched her with admiration. Music seeped into everything, strumming in her soul, coloring the aftertaste of wine on her tongue.

Someone jostled Dorottya, waking her from the vision. She had been staring.

A hefty man loomed. "Pig's ass," he sneered. "What's wrong with your face?" He took a drink from his mug and spit at her feet.

They'll see and hate you. Everyone will hate you.

Dorottya sneered back, struggling to hide her fear and shame. He had already turned away, the shirt on his broad back touched with perspiration, half stumbling toward the wine casks. She touched her face, fingertips moving over familiar lumps and blemishes. It *was* wrong, this flesh she wore. The music paused in some new anticipation. Villagers cleared and murmured.

Horrid to look upon.

The crowd parted as a line of girls, linked arm-to-arm, danced into the center. They wore white country dresses, ribbons streaming from their waists and hair. They smiled radiantly and moved in unison over the earth, ribbons floating around their bodies, making colorful circles and jagged lines through the air.

To Dorottya, it seemed their faces melted and reformed into masks, forever smiling, flowered and laced, bloodless effigies on the altar of beauty. Music vibrated like metallic bees, burrowing deep into the center of her mind, moving her to join the dance. Dorottya obeyed, becoming one with the glorious movement of perfection.

4

The interrogator asked, "Why would Erszébet, a beautiful noblewoman, consume pain as if it was the same as medicine?"

"It was medicine," she said.

Once, the Countess Erszébet, too ill to rise from bed, had a girl brought and tied down alongside her. The noble and the peasant laid together, breast to breast, hips to hips. A pretty doll, a fragile comfort. Eventually it would break, from old age or death or suffering. When the countess sunk her teeth into the captive flesh, chunks of peasant porcelain fell away, turning the doll into something writhing, shrieking and human.

Within every statue there is only raw stone.

She asked, "Have you ever seen a lovely girl weep?"

The interrogator shifted in his seat. "You are here to answer my questions."

He thinks questions are power but it only reveals that he is lacking, seeking and lost, poking aimlessly like a key in the dark, prodding for the relief of a lock to release. They pursue and in the end, it will be flames.

—

Shadows settled over Écsed castle, smothering the commotion that had moved through the halls like bats, flapping in discordant directions. The sauces on Susanna's plate had cooled and begun their unappetizing transformation into congealed globs. Her stomach twisted and she set her fork down helplessly. Erszébet's plate and chair sat empty across from Susanna, her youthful charge having eaten heartily and now lay stretched across her bed in the rhythmic whisper of sleep.

Susanna sucked in a breath.

The funeral would be quiet and done quickly. Erszébet's father, Lord Báthory, would see to that. The servants would be paid for their silence and the walls of Écsed would swallow the story of the chamberlain's dead daughter. Sweet child, a well-suited playmate for Erszébet, the two had practically been raised together. Next year, no one would remember the girl's name in public, not even her father.

Elena.

Susanna wiped her eyes.

This Báthory child, who slept so heavily that candle light strained to escape her, a girl Susanna had raised from breast to near womanhood, dreamed on as if the day had been a satisfying one. Acid burned in Susanna's empty stomach and she squeezed her eyes shut with a silent cry.

She had been the one to find the chamberlain's daughter contorted on the library floor, a raw memory that would haunt her always. Next to the poor child's body, an iron poker, glistening with baptismal dew. Elena's face hemorrhaged a mass of bruises, lips like moldy apples, a skull of swollen lumps. Only the child's dress was recognizable, embroidered blue flowers, stitched by a delicate hand.

Susanna had found Erszébet in a nearby chair, engrossed in some lesson on Greek letters, her quill scratching maddeningly against parchment. Flecks of dried blood had decorated the bridge of the girl's nose in a mockery of freckles. Fingernails caked with more evidence of her transgression, crescent moons of blackened scarlet.

Scratch, dip, tap.

A chill started at the base of Susanna's spine and spread like icy fingertips to her neck and around her heart. She had nursed this child, loved her as her own. Kissed bruised toddler knees. Taught her prayers and hymns. Inside the girl, there had to be something of that love, imprisoned in cruelty and in need of nurturing. Soon the girl would start her monthly blood and she'd need assurances then, and guidance. She'd still need a mother.

Susanna opened her eyes, away from the images in her mind. Erzsébet stirred in her sleep and the coverlets rippled in fabric waves. Above the bed, a tapestry of the Báthory dragon snaked along the wall, bearing its three great teeth piercing a globe of crimson. Susanna couldn't think of a better symbol for this child she had raised.

—

The carriage swayed along the dirt path. They were two days out of Écsed and already the journey had grown tiresome and monotonous. Before the Ottomans and Habsburgs, when Hungary ruled itself, it would have taken three days of steady travel to reach Sárvár. Many barriers now stood in the way, roads in disrepair, incursions of Ottomans, Habsburg political divisions, and peasant uprisings. To go around some regions rather than through made for safer traveling.

Susanna fingered the coins sewn into her skirt. Lord Báthory had paid her well to accompany Erzsébet, to join his daughter's new household. She would have gone anyway, despite how much she wished to leave the family's service. What mother abandons her child? Even a child capable of things such as this?

What mother is paid to be a mother?

A knock sounded overhead and Susanna knocked back, a wordless greeting. She managed to convince Lord Báthory to not only send her, but to allow her brother, Ficzkó, a useful hand and a good carriage driver, to accompany them as well. His presence comforted her in the same way a bottle of wine did for a drunk.

Erzsébet had thrown open the curtain and stared out glumly. The view of fields and scrub met the girl without enticement. Even the spring hadn't done much to clear the clouds of her worry. Susanna couldn't escape the feeling that despite the fourteen years she had spent with the Báthory household, she no longer knew Erzsébet.

How did those years go by so quickly?

Susanna had come into service as Erzsébet's nurse when the girl was barely a week old. She had still been young herself, barely older than Erzsébet now. The memory stung. No matter how young the mother or how many years had passed, the pain of losing a child never faded. Her own babe had been a month old, born a bastard, but no sin clung to him despite what the old and new Churches said, unmarred and perfect as the sunrise on a spring morning. Everything Susanna had been died with him, until Lady Báthory requested her service as a wet nurse for her newborn daughter, promising work for both her and her brother, Ficzkó. Somehow, her son's death gave her an opportunity for which they could have never hoped. Shifting her love to the Báthory child, her charge became life. In many ways, Susanna was the only mother the noble girl had known. Erzsébet's mother, even before she passed, had little interest in her own children.

Susanna could not abandon Erzsébet, despite what had happened. Yet Elena's mashed and swollen face loomed in her memory. Delicately embroidered flowers ensanguined with crimson suffering.

"He thinks I'm a monster," Erzsébet said, slicing and multiplying the tension.

Susanna's heart caught in her throat, suddenly ashamed of the coins. She chose her words carefully. "Your father keeps his plans to himself."

"You know very well he's sending me away."

"My lady," Susanna paused, "many noble girls marry at young ages. You've been promised to the Ferenc Nádasdy since you were barely old enough to walk."

Erzsébet swung her shadowy eyes away from the carriage window, her face drooped, the corners of her mouth downturned. "Elena . . . I miss her," she whispered. "I don't want to be a monster." The child's voice broke.

Sweet dear one, the babe she once held close, worrying through fevers, Susanna reached for the girl and gripped her with all the hope she could muster. Yet no words of refusal could rise to her lips. How could she ever think this child a monster? How could she ever think this child anything *but* a monster?

"I can't do this alone."

"Perhaps." Susanna's voice escaped stale as if bottled for too long. "It will be grace that meets us at the end of this journey."

—

When they spotted the hulking pitiful woman, a heavy rain had just broken over the road threatening to halt their journey for the day. The woman's skirts clung to her legs almost obscenely, her long hair a river of brown snaking over her face. She looked as miserable as the others of the retinue who had no carriage to cover them from the elements. Erzsébet had been stifling a yawn when her face lit up at the sight.

"Stop," she demanded from the carriage. "Bring that woman to me."

Puzzled, Susanna straightened in her seat. "My lady, what are you doing?"

"Grace, dear nurse."

"Grace?"

"Yes. I don't wish to wait for it to find me. Let us bring it with us from the beginning."

5

The interrogator wanted to know more.

It was not possible to know everything. How does one confess to the joy it brought when the girls were beaten? Or, the look in one's own eyes reflected through their terror? The honey of power? Could words explain what it was like to destroy something, only to realize you've destroyed everything?

—

"Good God, what sad mare bred you?"

"Is that a woman?"

"Nah, a troll."

They laughed.

"Maybe it can't talk," another man said, pointing with a gloved hand.

They'll see you and hate you.

"Can't she do something to make herself less painful to the eyes?"

Horrid. Horrid. Horrid to look upon.

"Some rouge, anything really."

"Nothing can help that."

"A sack over its face would help."

More laughter.

Two stomps, clap, twirl, jump. The fiddle played on although the festival had stopped. The maid of spring had been crowned, fields fertilized with her loveliness. Never Dorottya. She would have fouled the fields and cursed the harvests. Gathering around the maid, the villagers venerated their queen with smiles and early wildflowers. Dorottya though, they only spoke to in quips and sneers, their laugher eating away her senses.

Rain came down all at once, as if the clouds were a cracked egg, and the road before her waited to feel the tread of her boots upon its surface. A small voice within reminded that she needed shelter, the villagers had refused to share bread and salt. Do not welcome a stranger, such a horrid thing, born of the devil. Dorottya didn't disagree. A drum beat inside her mind, driving her to move. To where, she did not know.

Mother had taught her many things. Healing herbs and the telling of fortunes. How to cover her face to make the blows less damaging. How to cower.

Funny, one would think that she could know her own fortune.

———

She hadn't heard the horses and carriage, too many voices and colors blurred and overlapped, streaming into the attenuation of the droplets in their fall to the earth. She had watched the girls for a long time in the village. Dorottya hummed and her feet asked again to take flight, dwelling amongst them. More than that, she wished dearly to be them. For the interplay of adoring glances. Fair and perfect. A queen of fertility.

The dragon teeth banners stopped her in the mud, pushed her out of the jeers, flashing smiles and ribboned hair. A door opened from a gilded carriage. When she stepped inside, voices and colors unified and their edges defined. She understood, in that moment, the small noble girl seated within was the source of all the melodies of the world.

Dorottya never wanted to be far from that source ever again.

6

Girls have poisoned themselves in the pursuit of beauty, drowned in the need for perfection. Just to obtain some worth, because even a little worth is everything. It happened and it will happen again and again.

"How many years does a girl have? I know, you are the one who asks the questions here. But you have asked how many girls and before I can answer, I must know your answer—how many years does a girl have?"

"Enough. The Palatine will want to know why. All of Hungary will want to know why."

"Shhhhh."

Listen.

The answers are inside the walls.

———

Ferenc stifled a yawn as Reverend Magyari warmed to today's lesson. Truthfully, it had gone off course, rambling through off topics and stories of his youth. Stalwart in pretending he hadn't heard the whole mess a hundred times, Ferenc let his mind wander to large liquid eyes and crimson lips, the shape and curves under tailored gowns, loose lacings of maids, leaning to their work, cream legs protruding and enticing.

He hadn't noticed that Magyari had gone quiet. Ferenc's imagination galloped to war and enjoyed well-earned spoils. A warm hand clapped over his shoulder.

"Marriage is a big moment in a man's life," Magyari said, misunderstanding Ferenc's distraction. "We all know. That's why your mother sent me to here, to prepare you."

Ferenc shrugged, relieved he wouldn't have to explain himself.

"This is a good time for a new lesson." Magyari's voice sounded understanding, even compassionate.

Ferenc stifled a groan with deft experience. Appearances were the currency of political gain and one never knew where those advantages could sprout. He sat up and forced himself to attentiveness.

"My apologies sir—

Magyari held up a hand and took a seat in one of the cushioned chairs, a sigh of relief escaped him like a foul wind after a big meal. The reverend was not a particularly old man, slightly overripe in age but still prime. The man should be out in the wind on horseback, remembering the call of their ancestors, not leading this soft indoor life.

"Let me tell you, there are many things to learn about marriage. Unfortunately, most of it you'll have to learn on your own." The reverend leveled his gaze. He seemed to want Ferenc to take him terribly serious. "I can calm your nerves on this one thing, I hear your betrothed is a beautiful girl," he licked his lips, "and that means she is favored by God."

This surprised Ferenc. He had expected Magyari to launch into the history of clergy marriage in both the Church of Rome and the Lutheran Church, not point to the lust-worthiness of his betrothed. Ferenc almost laughed out loud.

"The Lady Báthory is a most worthy wife," Ferenc said noncommittally.

"I'm talking about her purity, you must understand. In all my experiences with women, I've learned that a woman's ugliness is an affliction of the soul. Like oil rising to the surface." The man shifted.

All his experiences? Men like Magyari didn't get many experiences they didn't force or pay for, and his poor sop of a wife, well, who knew how many times he'd experienced the woman. Not a great beauty, but neither was she hard to look at in a pinch. He'd give the reverend that much.

"Wouldn't that make beauty—

"The evidence of a pure soul?"

Or, something corruptible with marriage and use. Oddly, the idea made sense, the women he'd seen approaching their middling years seemed to tire and deflate their blooms. Best enjoy it as much as possible, while it lasted. Maybe Magyari experienced every moment he could with that wife of his. Religious men devoted themselves to God on the tongue and to sin with—

"It is a great indication. But I do warn care, Satan comes in many dazzling disguises. But the homely woman, it is as if original sin lives in her flesh." Magyari cleared his throat.

"Thank you, Reverend, I will keep memory of your words." In truth, when Ferenc saw most women, he didn't see much above their neck, or deeper than their flesh.

A manservant entered the room, his steps rigid as if he was made of wood. Much of Vienna among the nobility were like that, stiff and formal. Service to the Habsburgs tended to breed discomfort. The streets were where real life happened. Ferenc's lips tingled, recalling the night before. Women who charged knew all the best ways to pleasure a man, like a master carpenter or stonemason. He'd go back tonight. He straightened his back irritably.

"What is it?"

The manservant bowed. "I have news," he said, in German, and held a parchment out.

Ferenc took it, unsealing it impatiently. The words swirled over the page and his heart sank. His betrothed, the young Lady Báthory would soon arrive at his estate of Sárvár. Much earlier than expected, a year earlier than expected.

His mother directed his return within the month, irritation rose like an itch in the center of his back. He wanted more time, to prepare, to wrap his head fully around the idea of marriage. Panic rose up in his chest and he pushed it down viciously, crumpling the parchment in his hand.

"Are you alright, my lord?" Magyari asked.

Ferenc looked up at him and frowned.

7

She is a fresh currant, heavy on the vine, the tender insides of a pomegranate, holding their flesh around them like a blanket, daring everyone to suck and taste. Poor Persephone, she had a season too. Hades only wanted her dewy. Everyone thinks the queen of the underworld ate the seeds. Wasn't so. She was the food and Hades the greedy one who ate and ate before plucking another.

"When did you know that her ladyship was committing these . . . offenses?"

"I always knew."

Sucked and plucked. Persephone gave Hades a stomachache and afterword—she was all needles.

—

Red.

That was the first thing Dorottya saw when she took Erszébet's hand. The color settled like a haze over the inside of the carriage and over the noble girl's face. Red seeped into the crevices of the lines on her palm. The lines ran into a multitude of branching scarlet rivers, bursting forth and feeding the air they breathed.

Dorottya glanced up at the pale oval of the noble girl's face.

Red.

"You will give birth," Dorottya said, haltingly, examining the lines that represented children. "What you bring forth will pour into the world and will be talked about for centuries."

"What else do you see?" Erszébet asked in hushed tones.

"You will find love"—a wave of vertigo hit Dorottya.

The red seeped behind her eyelids and the image of a hall filled with mirrors rose, in the center stood a throne, a crown made of cracked bones and gems rested upon it.

Dorottya fell into the scarlet mist as if pushed from a cliff. She fought, gasped for air, clutched at nothing. Then, she did a curious thing, she simply let go.

The red disappeared.

Erszébet pursed her lips together, eyes bright with astonishment. "You had a vision, didn't you?" Her voice trembled.

"I think . . ." Dorottya stammered. She'd never experienced a vision. Mother had described them. A bride beneath a veil, vivid yet unrealized. That's exactly what it had been. "Yes."

Erszébet leaned forward, her small body tense. While barely of the age to marry, intelligence burned hot and dangerous within her. "Tell me what you saw."

"I saw power, I saw you powerful." The words popped out before Dorottya could understand them or why they had fallen from her mouth in the first place.

The noble girl's dark eyes grew luminous. She nodded, as if she'd known all along what was coming and only wanted an acknowledgement. Her nurse, the blonde woman, hovered nearby, disapproval over her features.

"I'm traveling to Sárvár to be with the family of my betrothed."

Dorottya understood, she wanted to know her fate, traveling through the countryside into the unknown. A time of great change. Everyone wanted to know their fate at those moments, as if it would come upon them in an instant when they crossed some imaginary line. Fate never does that, instead it worms into lives like the slow settling of silt into a lake after a storm.

"I see you're alone." Erszébet took on a sad look. "I'm alone too, my mother passed not long ago. My father doesn't want me anymore. He's sending me away."

The heaviness in the noble girl's voice made Dorottya sad too, she wanted to bridge the loneliness.

"It doesn't matter." Erszébet shook her head with a sigh. "You should join us. I'm quite interested in fortune telling."

Her attendant placed a hand on Erszébet's shoulder, parental and gentle. "My lady, I'm not sure that would be for the best. We cannot—

"Bring a witch with us to my betrothed estates?" Erszébet finished and shrugged. "I suppose you're right, Susanna." She turned, the sharp intelligence stashed away. "You're quite lowly in station. But really, how can I reach grace if I don't help those less fortunate than I?"

Susanna's face drained of color. "That's not quite what I meant."

"Then what did you mean?" Erszébet turned back to Dorottya. "What else do you see? Can you"—her voice pitched higher. The whites of her eyes shone. Violent tremors passed through her body and her bones shifted and begged for release from the flesh.

Dorottya froze as if movement would release the noble girl's skeleton, leaving behind the crimson insides of the child in a heap of scarlet ribbons.

Erszébet dropped to the floor of the carriage.

Susanna went to her knees, holding Erszébet's writhing form close. "She's in a fit," she called frantically to the men outside.

The coachman pulled at the door before the soldiers had a chance to react. Erszébet's small, booted feet twitched and kicked.

"Pull her out, she needs air," Susanna directed.

The coachman moved without question, scooped up the girl and laid her with surprising gentleness on the wet road. A young, cultivated product of power reduced to this seemed a shame, hair disheveled, frothing and veins protruding from abruptly sallow skin—in the mud of a lonely country road.

Without thinking, Dorottya moved to assist. When Erszébet made a soft choking sound, Dorottya tilted the noble girl's head and allowed the stream of foam to escape her mouth, freeing the airway. The dragon banners fluttered above them in a mockery of the scene. A young, frightened noble, helpless and small, surrounded by these men and their horses and their weapons, fate had surely beckoned Dorottya to this place. Healers pedaled their craft among the unfortunate, but for those with both wealth and illness, healers were wanted more than pretty dresses or new estates.

Susanna scooped the still twitching Erszébet away from Dorottya, the attendant's eyes filled with suspicion and fear. "We have to wait it out," she explained.

Holding the child tenderly, the woman sang, tears in her eyes, expensive gown rumpled and mudded around her. She didn't seem to notice.

The twitches slowed and Erszébet took frantic gulps, sucked in air and particles of the dirt that had flecked along her lips.

Awareness, albeit faint, returned and Erszébet lifted her head weakly. Susanna leaned back against the wheel of the carriage, still holding the girl, and exhaled with relief.

"The falling sickness," she said, as if explaining to the air.

Dorottya realized that she had been wringing her hands in her skirts. Her mind went to the things her mother had told her about varying illnesses. "I have medicine," she said. "If you will permit me, I cannot cure the sickness but can treat the pain in the head that happens after."

Susanna looked surprised.

The coachman grinned. "Witch, eh? Aren't we in luck. That would be lovely, really lovely. Little ladyship gets the pain in her eyes bad after a fit." Compact and tawny, the coachman's black hair grew in random directions that gave him a carefree air. Despite a significant contrast between the two, a certain resemblance made Dorottya wonder if he was some relation to the nurse.

This same nurse, whose look of suspicion had settled over her features like a shadow, paused before finally nodding in cautious agreement.

Erszébet had squeezed her eyes shut, threading her fists onto Susanna's sleeves, and moaned in pain. Horses around them nickered and men shuffled uneasily.

"Here, my lady." Dorottya pushed a small bottle forward. "Drink it in small sips, no more than two at a time. It is quite strong."

The nurse unstopped the bottle and took a whiff. "What's in it?"

"Mostly lavender, madam." She didn't lie, but didn't mention the other ingredients, small amounts of substances used in ways

28

only mother taught. She didn't think they'd know most of it anyway. Her best mixture yet, and it worked. It could kill most pain for a day or more. "Only two sips, my ladyship, more could be dangerous," she warned. It was also quite addictive.

The nurse eyed the tincture with doubt, glancing at the small, tight fists on her sleeves, her charge turned inward and curled into a ball. The woman softened. Dorottya thought she saw tears.

"I'll try it." the coachman stepped forward. He gave a kind glance in Dorotttya's direction. "Don't think we have anything to worry about, but I'm happy to calm nerves if it'll get our ladyship some relief."

He took a swig and gave a satisfied grin. "Let's get Lady Báthory back inside."

Susanna and the coachman worked together, creating a makeshift bed from a multitude of cloaks on the floor of the carriage. Eyes squeezed shut against the pain, Erszébet let out quiet whimpers as they moved her. Soldiers stood around as if interrupted in play, quiet, awkward and utterly useless. Perhaps they were not regulars of the noble household.

The coachman stood abruptly.

"What is it?" The nurse asked.

"Well, I'll be damned." The coachman gave Dorottya a look of respect. "My leg's been aching for weeks, but I swear, just like that, it's gone."

Dorottya tried not to let her crooked teeth show through her grin of pride. She knew the tincture worked, but more than that, someone had looked at her with something other than a smirk, believed in her without judgement—acted with kindness to her. A blush bloomed.

"It'll be a great help to the lady," the coachman added.

The encouragement pierced through Susanna's cold exterior and she softened. "Here my lady, try it as the witch says, no more than two sips."

They propped up the Erszébet to drink. She lapped like a weak kitten before huddling back into her tortured haze.

Without turning to Dorottya, the nurse mumbled, "Thank you." But Dorottya had heard it. Whether it was meant for her or God, she didn't care. She'd found where she belonged.

Erszébet turned in her makeshift bed, peering at Dorottya with wonder, a gentle smile curved her lips. "It's gone," she said. "The pain in my head, it has gone. Like a storm receding." Erszébet turned to her nurse. "See, even if my father won't forgive me, God can. He's sent me a healer."

A sense of victory surged through Dorottya. *Do you see me, mother? I'm worth something more than pretty dresses and new estates. It doesn't matter what I look like. I'm wanted and you were wrong all along.*

The constant echo inside her skull responded, but this time Dorottya refused to listen.

8

Stone and brick are the cloak of dark deeds.

Made by man and the deeds committed by man. They don't say "woman." Because the female is a gentle thing, motherhood and love. Devils when they spurn him though. Temptresses. Foul Liliths.

"Human flesh is a wonderful cloak."

The interrogator stares. If he could, he'd nibble his nails and swallow the little jagged edges. Not sure which words are said aloud or within anymore. Did he hear that one? Well, it is the truth. Hide all the darkness and ugliness inside the folds of another. Pretending and agreeing to allow everyone their false covers.

"Just like stone, you know."

He is writing, thinking of another question. Formulating and planning. Building his own little wall with the words of people, written on the skins of animals.

———

Arrival in Sárvár was not what Susanna hoped it would be.

She expected the Nádasdy's to send out riders, emissaries of welcome. Not necessary, yet customary, especially when greeting members of high-ranking families such as the Báthory's, a name

31

associated with power. While Hungary struggled under the strain of the Habsburg-Ottoman tug-of-war, what power left to the region resided within the branches of the Báthory family. Susanna's charge embodied the union between her parents, Anna and George, whose marriage and issue brought together the branches of the family. At times, Susanna wondered if the they shared too close of relation by blood for the sake of healthy children, at least when it came to sound minds. Heat infused her cheeks, she could hear Ficzkó outside, the all-too familiar sound of his voice commanding the horses. She knew some of what can happen when a child's parents shared too much of the same blood.

It would not be like that for Erszébet, she'd ensure the girl found her way.

When they sent out riders to announce their impending arrival, the men did not return. No welcoming host came to greet them. The carriage simply creaked forward unceremoniously into the jaws the castle, gobbled up like a daily meal.

Erszébet pretended to not notice the slight, focusing instead on picking the mind of the newest member of her employ, this witch. The corners of Susanna's mouth tugged down. An ugly thing, she thought, more creature than human. That must have added to the allure of the unknown for Erszébet, as if the significance of appearance marked power.

More likely it marked a marred soul, fissured by the devil. Anything but grace.

While Erszébet no longer complained of headaches, she too often pressed that tiny bottle to her lips, imbibing surreptitious nips of the brew. At least there had not been another episode… yet. A poor thing indeed if her charge met her new home with thrashing and a foaming mouth.

Only the business of the day met them in the courtyard, staff going about their errands and work, necessary for running a castle. The baroness, Lady Nádasdy had been widowed long before and she had a particular reputation for efficiency, one that had clearly been an accurate description. There seemed a joylessness about the place, a monotonous existence of responsibility.

"Please wait here, someone will be along to fetch you," Susanna directed, and pressed a coin into the witch's palm, trying not to wince at the close contact. "It is not seemly for you to accompany us." Partial truths razored her tongue. With any luck, the witch, forced to wait too long, would search elsewhere for employ.

Susanna and Erszébet were shown to their apartments in the eastern wing of the castle by a dour manservant eager to be rid of them. Well-furnished rooms dotted the corridor, befitting the stature of a noble girl in the family estate of her betrothed. Stale air begged for open shutters as some rooms had been tidied for Erszébet's use, yet a good number remained cluttered, storing furniture and other dusty curiosities. While the wing belonged to Erszébet in name, functionally it would not accommodate a retinue size befitting her station.

The end of the haphazard journey and the clear spring day signaled a new start and Susanna tried to conjure good humor despite her misgivings. She swept into the main chamber, opened windows, and inspected the bedding and various fixtures. Good quality and handsomely decorated. Susanna noted the large bookshelf, already boasting books in many languages and topics, all things she would include in her report to Lord Báthory. Not that he would be overly concerned for Erszébet's comfort, but the appearance of such and, by extension, regard to the Báthory name.

They splashed their faces with water, wiping away the dirt of long travel, and dusted their gowns. Golden sunshine peeked into the room and lit Erszébet's unbound chesnut waves. Susanna remembered the first time she held the girl, all sweetness in the daylight. When night fell, the babe wailed as if, without sunshine, she could not find her own fingers to suck. Susanna cared for the child in an isolated nursery rarely visited by the nobles, the Báthory's being more concerned about wars and new political alliances. No tenderness or kindness in the hearts of the powerful.

Susanna's throat caught and she gathered the girl up into a fierce embrace.

Erszébet drooped in her arms. "Do you think they will like me?"

Just a girl, Susanna thought, unsure and frightened. She gulped down sorrow and worry with the question. She hoped that the Nádasdy's had not heard of Erszébet's violent episode and to a lesser extent, the fits.

Unlikely.

The baroness was a thorough woman, there would be little she didn't examine when it came to her son and the future of the only heir to the Nádasdy estates.

"You are beautiful and of good breeding, better than theirs. If they do not, then they are fools and you will be baroness someday." Susanna cupped Erszébet's face, giving the girl all the love she could muster. The girl's eyes had grown deeper and filled with longer shadows each passing season and no matter what Susanna did, she could not beat it back. Now those eyes bubbled with pain and fear and, worst of all, a dark thing made from the vinegar of her short life.

"I love you as if I birthed you myself," Susanna said. Tears stung her eyes. "You've done everything to prepare for this moment and the moments to come. You are strong, now is the time for strength over any obstacles you face."

Erszébet nodded and a frown pulled down the corners of her mouth.

A knock came at the door.

Erszébet pulled away. At once, a cold haughtiness emanated from her. A noble girl and her commoner nurse, nothing more. Susanna wiped her face and went to answer.

"Baroness Nádasdy will receive Lady Báthory in the meeting hall," a servant said.

"Already? We haven't a chance to refresh ourselves." Susanna cast a glance behind her.

Erszébet strode forward, her face made of stone, ignoring Susanna's protest. "Lead the way, sir."

9

"Hitting and spitting."

He nodded scribbling. "That's how they all started?"

What an odd thing. How did they start to die? No different than life for anyone. First beaten, but it isn't the single blows that begins to kill, it is the accumulation and the lack of time for the flesh to recover. Mouthfuls of fat and muscle ripped, chewed and swallowed to nourish the darkness in another. No one asks how they started to live.

A key and a lock, my friend.

The question . . . the interrogator expects an answer. He had stopped scribbling. A gaping pore on his nose threatening to swallow anything too close. A pit to the underworld, where the answer lies. It would boil up into a fine puss-filled blemish soon.

So ugly.

"Sometimes. Other times, needles."

———

Dorottya had been told to wait, and she would.

A mist enveloped the cobbled causeway and above loomed towers that Dorottya imagined were the dancing girls from the village, their pale skin topped with red roofs, their dark windows staring down at the new arrivals. The castle breathed around her, slow and sure of itself, a sturdy and dirty old man.

Voices and footfalls echoed from an open window above. She imagined a great hall from which they emanated, the paintings and tapestries that must fill it and the fine important people who lived there. She caught snippets of words.

"A mere child."

"Young, but that is good," another answered. "Will be humbled."

"Fair as her portrait?"

"She's a Báthory."

The voices floated away.

Most of the soldiers were gone, the work completed. How long had she waited?

"And who the hell are you?" A middle-aged woman loomed over Dorottya. Broad hands rested disapprovingly on her hips. Curt and cut from country stock, the woman wore a simple but well-pressed frock, her graying hair pulled into a tight low bun.

"I came with her Ladyship Báthory."

"I asked who the hell you are, not your ladyship. I know who she is, but you look like a fish sucking air."

"Dorottya."

"Dorottya what?"

"Dorottya Széntes."

The woman sniffed. "Oh God, you stink. What do you do exactly, Dorottya?"

"I am a healer."

The woman's eyes narrowed.

"Her ladyship gets headaches."

The woman assessed Dorottya closely in the awkward silence.

"We've no use for a healer now," she said.

Dorottya stood, smoothing her skirts. "Not now, but you will need one sometime." The confidence in her voice surprised her, invigorated her.

"We have healers to call on in town." The woman frowned. "You'd only be an extra expense. We don't need extra expenses."

"I can work," Dorottya said. Susanna never meant to come back for her. The nurse didn't want her here. Nor did the woman trust her.

Mocking laughter echoed in Dorottya's mind.

"Doing what?"

"I can . . ." What could she do? What did she have to offer? She'd never worked in a castle before or served a noble. Dorottya straightened. "Whatever is needed."

Something in the woman's curt face softened. "Nowhere to go, eh?"

Dorottya shook her head. "My mother's died."

Silence. The woman peered at Dorottya. "The bathhouse needs a hand. Warning you though, not easy work there. The baroness likes things a certain way. No holidays."

Dorottya's pride drained away. "I can do it. I'm used to hard work."

"Fine. You're a wash maid now."

"Wash maid?"

"Washerwoman, dear God, stupid woman. Take yourself and your healing to the bathhouse. Your work is there." The woman pointed to a door.

Dorottya belonged here.

"And wash yourself and your clothes while you are there. Can't have a reeking pile of bumpy flesh wandering the castle."

Dorottya bustled through door and into an area undoubtedly visited only by the servants. Exposed brick held up the castle floors above and already dampness sunk into the air. Following the dim corridor toward the thickening wet air, she almost bumped into a large tarnished mirror hung at the end of the hall. Her own image stared back at her.

A thing.

She'd seen her reflection in streams, ripples blurring her features together, making the depth of her appearance, the sheer offense of it, muddled. Never looked into a true mirror, not like this.

Lumped colorless flesh, too-full lips like rotted liver against dark-stained teeth. Thin hair clutched to her scalp in claw-like desperation.

The eyes were the worst. She had thought that perhaps, even if she was without beauty, her soul would shine through those eyes, but her mother had managed to ruin even that. The flesh puckered and scarred around one from—Not now, no more memories. Free now from mother, free and serving a noble lady.

The dingy brown of her irises looked like used oil. They seemed to disagree.

Her breath came out in a loud whoosh.

Not a monster, but her own face.

A revolting thing, pockets of pus threatening to burst open the truth.

Ugliest I've ever seen.

Horrid. Horrid. Horrid to look upon.

They'll see you and hate you.

—

Those found beyond the eastern wing were blurs of movement, only servants, well dressed and kept. Each dedicated to a task—hauling linens, sweeping, painting whitewash to the stucco walls. So much of the castle existed as tidy tomes of expensive objects, only beheld by the servants who maintained them.

The manservant led Susanna and Erszébet down a windowed walkway. Men worked in the courtyard below, unloading the personal items and supplies they had brought with them from Écsed. Erszébet had not taken much with her, mostly gowns, but also several books from the Écsed collection that she cherished. The shelf in her chamber would be put to good studious use.

They were led into a shadowed hall. Most of the shutters here remained closed and waited for a time to display Nádasdy wealth to worthy visitors. It did not seem that Erszébet was counted among that number. The floors, made of fine inlaid woods swirled together, created designs in the language of dead trees. Paintings ran along the walls of Nádasdy ancestors, scenes from history and the Bible, yet even with all these details Susanna almost laughed. Sárvár might be closer to the heart of Habsburg power of Vienna, but it still could not match the wealth of the Báthory estates.

Erszébet looked appropriately unimpressed, even when she glimpsed Lady Nádasdy accompanied by her son. The pair waited as if they were royalty receiving a vassal's petition.

Neither turned their placid faces toward their visitors. Susanna bristled.

Haughty and distant, nobles to the core, Lady Nádasdy wore her hair tightly pulled from her forehead and tucked neatly under a cap. Ferenc, the prized heir, was a barrel of a young man, his beard grew with the intensity of someone older, and this he kept trimmed short around his mouth like a picture frame.

The manservant stepped forward, gesturing in rigid formality. "My lord and lady, I present Lady Báthory, as requested."

Only then did the pair turn their attention. Ferenc gave nothing away, his intensity settled on Erszébet like one assessing the value of a horse.

"Lady Báthory, it is God's blessing that we finally lay eyes on you after many years." The baroness said. "You may not remember, but I have visited and supped with your father in Écsed."

"I'm sorry, my lady, I do not recall but I am pleased to be seen." Erszébet knew this game too well.

"I had heard that you were ill during your journey. I hope you are recovered." Ferenc smirked.

So they knew. But how much? Did they know that this child could fall writhing to the ground at any moment?

"I am, my lord," Erszébet responded. "It is a pity there was no one of the Nádasdy household to accompany me once we reached your lands. My health would have been better cared for."

Susanna held her gaze to the floor, following the loops and turns of the design, wishing for invisibility. Had she been Erszébet's mother, she would have rebuked the girl.

"You keep company too much with commoners, it is no wonder you've learned such gruff manners. No matter. We shall see to it that you are taught better. I have arranged a special tutor for you," Lady Nádasdy said, eyes flashing. "It is no small thing to run a household. I intend that you know everything before you wed."

"I've had the best teachers already in Écsed. Perhaps you have forgotten my family name," Erszébet answered. Susanna resisted the urge to yank her charge out of the room for a stern discussion.

Lady Nádasdy's eyes grew hostile and the mood of the room seemed to further dim. "You have a lot to learn. First lesson is that this is not Écsed and we act and speak appropriately in Sárvár."

Erszébet did not retort and Susanna let out a sigh. The girl threw her head back proudly and bowed deeply to Ferenc. "I am pleased to finally meet with my betrothed. I have heard you are a ferocious fighter. Surely you will push the Ottomans finally out of Hungary." With a smile she added, more quietly, "Perhaps the Habsburgs too."

The Nádasdy heir bowed in response. "Thank you for your confidence, my lady. That is my hope."

The girl gazed at him through her lashes, the look of an amorous woman. "I would love to hear the stories of your training. Do you enjoy the hunt? I hope so, I brought riding gowns."

Clever girl, Susanna thought. Lady Nádasdy brought her hands to her stomach as if holding back outrage. A prickly woman and not one worth offending. Yes, clever but also foolish, Erszébet.

"I . . ." Ferenc began. His mustache twitched. "Unfortunately, I will not have that honor for some time. I must return to school in Vienna."

"Oh." Erszébet's face fell, a child again. "How long, my lord?"

"My son will be deep in his studies until next spring." Lady Nádasdy said. "At which point you will wed, if I feel you are ready. My son will need a proper manager of the estate, someone with a firm hand and a good head."

Erszébet pursed her lips.

"If I may, my lord, my lady," Susanna said, keeping her gaze lowered. "Lady Báthory is young but is quite accomplished and I think you will find any lessons that are given, she will learn all there is to know dutifully."

"Good," Lady Nádasdy said. "I will hold you to that promise. I will send Reverend Magyari to your chamber just after midday. We will have your meals brought to you, unless otherwise specified. You may go now."

Ferenc did not appear displeased at the tone his mother had taken with his betrothed. He shifted his attention to the window. The world called to him. A man of the outdoors, no wonder his mother sought so ardently to educate his future wife, she knew her son would be a rare sight at the castle. Susanna's heart sank a little. Not the change she had hoped for Erszébet— more solitude, time locked away within a chamber and trapped within lessons of German or Latin or courtesies of greeting or how to pray for her own sinful soul.

No, this was not where Erszébet would flourish.

10

They built a pyre outside. It would be lit and all the fat would melt into bubbling oil. The wood knocked against the stone, insisting entry, tapping out codes that all spelled . . .

P-E-R-F-E-C-T.

This is how to be beautiful:

Hair must be brushed with one hundred strokes each night. Or fifty-five. Three hundred.

Eat enough so that the body becomes like the soft hills of the Hungarian landscape, pleasant and enticing, but not too much that the body becomes a jellyfish. At that point there should be no food for two days.

Lift the breasts high, but not so high that they tower over the men. They do not like it if a woman is taller than them. So shrink.

Be young. Never ever grow old.

Don't live, don't breed without permission, but always give pleasure.

—

May, 1573

Most of the verbal assaults came along with showers of spittle from the manservants and guards. But women in their silence

41

and exclusion stung the most. Women who kept their whispers to corners, filling the cracks with stifled laughter and unspoken insults. The silence clouded with sneers until Dorottya thought it would smother her. When not washing, Dorottya drew water and delivered jugs throughout the castle. Cumbersome and heavy, the jugs were a bane, sapping strength and leaving her body aching.

In the evenings, she brewed bottles of the tincture that kept Erszébet's pain at bay and each morning Ficzkó came for the next bottle, but never to summon Dorottya to serve his lady.

Built into the base of the eastern defensive wall, Dorottya had stumbled upon a small room, a hole of a place that must have once served as storage. With easy access to the surrounding woodlands and castle gardens, Dorottya settled into the space and blended herbs for a variety of ailments. It seemed right that she should burrow herself here, inside a dancing girl, watching from vacant sockets.

The walls folded around her and whispered comfort and welcome.

Ficzkó had arrived. If only she could fold around him, they'd all be one, the walls, her and this man.

"Lovely morning," he said, his voice warm.

Dorottya gathered the newest bottle. "Please warn her ladyship to use this sparingly." The supply of the herb needed to brew the tincture had already dwindled alarmingly.

"I've tried," he laughed. "Can't give nobles commands though, they don't like anything that's not their idea first."

"I've heard wives say the same about their husbands." Dorottya couldn't help but smile.

"Suppose it's not very different." Ficzkó ran a hand over his hair, the early morning sun turned his skin to dusty gold. How unlike his sister he seemed. The richness of his voice made Dorottya relax, pushed away the sounds of the dancing girls, the old man . . . mother.

"Thank you, Dory," Ficzkó said, leaning against the doorframe.

But soon enough he'd be gone and the others would return.

One of her mixtures from the night before dotted a table, dissected leaves, buds and seeds with trails of oozing sap. She popped the seeds into a dark bottle, shelving it. "I hope she listens," Dorottya said, almost to herself. Must find more of the herb. What if it only grew in the woods she grew-up in?

"Dory."

"Yes?" She turned.

"I never see you anywhere in the castle that Ilona hasn't sent you. Never at meals or—

"I eat here," she interrupted. "Alone."

Ficzkó stood straight and took a step forward. "That's what I mean. I know people aren't kind to you, but it doesn't mean you should be . . . alone."

She saw her mother in her mind. They had leaned over a stream together. Dorottya desperately tried to see herself in the water.

"No one can love that." Her mother pointed to the reflection.

"No momma, not true."

"The sooner you learn that, the better for you. Gotta get used to being alone."

"But you love me, don't you?"

Her mother had never answered.

Dorottya looked into Ficzkó's soft eyes. "It's safer here, alone." Her voice almost a whisper.

He shook his head.

Someone called his name and he looked out with a sudden devious expression. "I must go." Pocketing the tincture, he darted into the full sunshine with a wave.

"Goodbye," she whispered.

11

My Lord Father,
May God bless you. I am eager to hear some word from you.
As I wrote with my last letter, I have settled well into the castle
and have begun instruction as directed by the baroness. My days
are long behind walls of brick and filled with memorization of
wine barrels and timber needed for repairs. They send me to
learn Greek letters as if I am a child. I am not allowed to travel
outside the castle and am barely permitted in the courtyard. The
baroness has appointed a new maid to accompany me, of course,
but she is a wily thing and I regard her as nothing more than a
twittering spy. Without Susanna, I think I would be the loneliest
girl on this earth. Please send me news of your health.
May God keep you.
Your loyal daughter,
Erszébet

—

The chamber door shut with a soft thud and even a new day
could do little to bring cheer to Susanna. Her brother did that to
her, trapped her, yet he also made her feel less alone. It'd been
like that for as long as she could remember. Just like their father,
it hurt to watch, all charm and obsession. Making friends

everywhere he went while Susanna waited in the background.

But he never left her, she had to remember that. Ficzkó was as constant as a mountain.

She had never been charming. Quiet and shy, she only responded to others, reciting words and tones they'd find pleasing. Susanna soothed. Ficzkó conquered.

Then she birthed her son and a new instinct grew up loud within her. A wish for something more. Maybe that instinct had withered and died on the vine along with her son's life.

Susanna donned a shift and chose a gown for the day. She wondered how Erszébet's chamber maid, appointed by the Baroness Nádasdy, faired. Erszébet had made it her mission to drive the girl mad each morning out of resentment of her future mother-in-law. Go to her, she thought, check on her. She had to fight those instincts. Erszébet needed some independence away from an overbearing nurse. Susanna sat on the bed, her brother's scent still strong on the coverlet. Without someone to serve, purpose drained away.

Listless, she opted to wander, explore this new home and think. The unoccupied rooms of the upper level of the east wing were filled with curiosities and Susanna took to exploring them. Dust in the corners had accumulated for so long that layers created nests of neglect. Like her and Ficzkó. Once a lively thing, now only collecting life's sorrow together out of habit. She loved him, yet she had never been given any other option. Youth played a part and fear of a world without him. But Susanna had grown, faint lines sunk into the crossroads of her skin, loss ached in her soul. There could be more.

These rooms were still fine in their own forgotten way, rich brocaded curtains, lovely woodwork and beds still made as if ready to welcome guests. Susanna realized the rooms assigned to Erszébet must have been much the same before they arrived, a corner to shove and forget things of the past. This gave the wing a hollow atmosphere, as if a scream would only bounce from wall to wall and never escape, with no ears to ever hear it.She pushed cobwebs from a shelf, blowing on the dust and watching it dance into the air as if the tiny specs were brought to life. Underneath, she found a lady's ivory mirror. The shapes of women danced along the frame, carved swirls echoed their movement as if they sought to escape the surface upon which they were made.

Susanna gazed at her foggy reflection. Older, but not old yet, surely past the traditional age for marriage but there could be possibilities. Clear blue eyes may be still considered alluring. Erszébet wouldn't need her forever and then what would she do? The idea of settling in a village house with Ficzkó repulsed and drew her. A simple life, it would end like it started, the two of them together. He'd keep her like an old collected coin. At least she'd still have value.

One thing in the room appeared to have been recently cared for, a shelf lined with more volumes of priceless books. No surprise as Hungarians had the Nádasdy's to thank for bringing the practice of printed books to the kingdom. Though most people throughout the realm couldn't read, so she supposed they wouldn't thank the Nádasdy's for anything after all.

Drawn to a plain leather-bound tome, Susanna pulled it from its home, admiring the simple quality of its binding. The leather still bore striations and pores, giving memory that it once housed flesh and bone. It opened easily like a recently oiled hinge.

An old and familiar tale spilled on the pages. A young girl fled into the woods to escape a wicked witch. The jealous woman wanted to punish a young girl's beauty. The fool of a girl ate the poison offered to her, crunched it between her fine teeth until she dropped to the ground. But she was not dead, she was something else, a work of art hoovering between life and death, laid in a glass coffin.

Susanna turned the page. Here the story continued, but around the margins someone had clustered their own notes, letters looping and vying for space. It seemed nonsense, fragments of words and ideas. A chill went over her. The fragments gave way to one phrase, repeated over and over, looping and strangling the original text, finding every crevice to bleed into . . .

Fairest, fairest, fairest, fairest.

A blue demon bent over the words. His forked tongue snaked out in an obscene caress. Prickles of cold crept up Susanna's spine. She couldn't look away.

He reached for her, an ache of longing from her soul ignited. The fairest, loved above all others. A warmth stabbed her middle, a growing desire that only Ficzkó had ever been able to coax from her.

Loud voices in the hall shook her awake. Susanna slammed the book shut. Back through the dusty piles of finery, tripping over rugs from far away kingdoms, and tumbling from the room. Gasping, Susanna rocked on her wobbly legs.

"I warn you," a familiar voice yelled down the hall.

In front of her chamber, Erszébet, hair hanging in half disarray, emitted such loudness that seemed impossible to come from a demure girl of her size.

She shrieked at her cowering maid, "I will take the skin of your scalp the next time you pull my hair while dressing it."

The maid, Reka, nodded silently. Tears ran down her cheeks.

"Oh, thank God, Madam Susanna is here." Erszébet calmed at the sight of her nurse. "I cannot have this girl doing my tresses. She does it wrong and it hurts. She pulls and tugs until I swear my hair is being shorn from my head."

Dazed, Susanna tried to respond but Erszébet huffed, too frustrated to wait for slow thoughts.

"What do you have?" Erszébet asked.

Susanna peered down, she still held the mirror, the girls on the frame screaming for freedom.

Erszébet clapped her hands together. "It is beautiful. Give it to me."

A wave of nausea moved through the nurse, but did as she was bid. Just as she always had.

Delighted, the girl grasped it, running a hand lovingly over the carved faces of the women. They screamed at her touch. Erszébet turned it over. An inscription, etched onto the ivory like cuts into fine skin.

Susanna squeezed her eyes shut, she didn't want to know, didn't want to hear. But Erszébet's voice told her anyway, the words sizzling on her tongue and parting the air.

She read, "To the fairest."

Susanna saw the word behind her eyes, over and over, embroidered in pretty blue flowers.

Fairest, fairest, fairest, fairest . . .

12

People think it is one, just a single angry, sick, twisted person.

Little deaths, then bigger ones and then mortal life and then freedom from innocence. All the deaths build and people create kingdoms of it.

—

Men were cruel.

Sprawled like a swampy lump in the mud, Dorottya froze, an animal playing dead. Freshly laundered clothes, her morning's work, tumbled out of the basket like they had been regurgitated from a sick stomach.

"Slip did you?" A Nádasdy guard grunted behind a smirk. Two of his friends leaned against the wall behind him and snickered approval.

Dorottya hadn't slipped. She'd been shoved from behind. The castle inhaled, waiting to drink in another batch of suffering.

"Not much of a lady are you?" The guard kicked a sloppy splash of muck into her face. "Got nothing to say, witch?"

Ice settled into her stomach. "Please stop," she whispered, helplessly.

One of the washing maids crossed the courtyard, casting a careless glance at the muddy scene. Dorottya watched too, hips shifting in languid steps, the cream of her flesh pure.

Mirella. Pretty Mirella.

Mirella was a peach and, if Dorottya bit into her, she would surely be the same sweet, snow-white flesh beneath. Dorottya wanted just that, to bite, take her into herself, chewing and smacking her lips so the girl would be part of her ugliness. For ruin or worship. A time for both.

A guard followed Dorottya's stare and kicked at the mud again, splashing her already soaked skirts. "Wishing you were a woman, not a creature eh? Devil put tits on yah, but you're no woman."

Ugliest I've ever seen.

Horrid. Horrid. Horrid to look upon.

Mirella floated above the mud of the courtyard. The towers danced around her, framing the loveliness against gray skies.

"That there is what a real woman looks like," a guard said.

Tears were close. Weak tears.

They'll see you and hate you.

Someone pulled Dorottya to her feet. Warm hands, gentle.

"Come on," said Ficzkó in a quiet voice.

She had to focus on him, clutching his sleeve to make the man real. Mud smeared against him from her fingers.

"You alright?" He asked.

Sickened to see her own filth. Dorottya released him, a hasty reflex of shame. "Yes," she whispered.

A grim cast sharpened his features as he nodded, leaning down to gather the scattered bits of laundry.

One of the guards called out, "Witch lover."

Another guard laughed.

Ficzkó's face twisted in distaste but he paid them no further mind.

"Take your little witch and drown her. Don't need her kind here."

Ficzkó guided Dorottya away as she shivered from the wet mud, making her skirts stick to her legs in odd angles.

"Here," he said, passing the basket.

"Thank you." Close to a whimper, a child yelling for her mother to stop. No more hurting.

His eyes were so green, like the woods. So green . . . and filled with pity.

Dorottya's vision blurred and she turned away, running to some unknown place, anywhere to escape his look.

Salty tears and mud ran over each lump on her face.

—

Ferenc itched to return to Vienna, to rise out of this tomb. How can a castle seem small, he wondered, a whole world outside and this place doesn't look further than its own walls. Just a few more days and he could finally escape.

His mother ate slowly, chewing each bite with disciplined haughtiness. He wanted to stuff that mouth with the brocades she wore.

"I'd be honored to stay, my lady, and to continue conducting lessons." Reverend Magyari looked positively pleased with himself. Whenever excited, he licked his lips and it appeared that he'd been very excited as of late.

"Good. I knew that we could rely on your steadfastness." The baroness scooped up another slice of meat from her plate, giving a manservant a nod as he refilled her wine cup. "Lady Báthory will need the company," she said, her gaze still on the servant. "I've dismissed most of her household retinue. They should be well on their journey back home now."

"Have you? Cutting costs, I assume," Ferenc said.

"Oh yes," she warbled. "I'll allow her to keep the nurse and this man here. He's proven useful with information."

The manservant had the look of a laborer, a small swarthy fellow with an easy grin.

"Unless I've missed someone?" His mother wiped her mouth.

The manservant paused in his retreat to his station in a corner. "No lady, I don't believe you have." He bowed.

Satisfied, she turned her full attention to Ferenc, sharpening his longing for escape.

"How have you found your betrothed?" His mother's eyes had aged so much since his father died. Not much joy in her, even less now.

He resisted the urge to scrub a hand through his hair. "I haven't."

She arched an eyebrow and frowned.

"She is too young."

"And you are not?"

He bristled. "I am not a child. What do you expect me to do with her? Play dolls?" Ferenc clamped his mouth shut with surprise, a wave of relief came over him as if he had held those words within him for years and finally they had flown free.

Magyari had stopped licking his lips, falling into silence, his face pointed and twitchy like a mouse.

"Appearances are important, my son. If you haven't organized time to spend with her, then I expect you to lie about it."

"Lie?"

"Yes," the countess said. "I care little for the spoiled Báthory girl, but you know what her family brings to the Nádasdy name. Any appearance of fracture between our families weakens us. Granted, Lord Báthory has little desire to have the girl back, there is no love lost there—especially after what the little monster did before she got here." She sighed. "But, if it is said you don't like her, then there will be secret missives sent to her father suggesting other betrothals and alliances. He could ship her off to a new husband-to-be without having to see her at all. I'd rather avoid that."

Ferenc saw the value of this, working to secure the Nádasdy future, his future. A grudging respect grew. "I see."

"Good, I will write her father with news of what a wonderful match you two make."

"Truly, I couldn't be happier. She's delightful," he responded, his mouth dry.

Magyari resumed his meal, nibbling happily.

"You really are your father's son, sweet Ferenc." Her lips lifted upwards, for a moment she looked alive again, then it disappeared.

Soon, he would be gone too.

And God help him, he'd make it his mission to return as little as possible.

—

Reka put a hand on her friend Mirella's arm. They had taken to mending shirts in the courtyard. With the morning hours still chilly in the shadows, they kept to the sun, a delicious warmth that promised a lovely day.

"There she is," Reka whispered in the tone of conspiracy.

Mirella raised her eyes, meaning to pretend a casual glance. She looked for a moment too long, took in enough of the landscape and of the witch, Dorottya, that a sense of wrongness perforated her own being in response. The witch set down a large jug, arms gangly at her sides. Detecting the stare, her mouth twisted in disdain at finding the source.

Mirella looked away. "Stop gossiping," she told Reka.

"Me?" Reka laughed, throwing off the irritated edge of Mirella's voice.

Contagious flippancy. Reka was contagious.

"You're so innocent, Mirella. I'm here to educate you."

The ugly witch had moved on, but Mirella's cheeks still bloomed with heat.

"The woman deals in black magic. I'm told she was picked up during the journey from Écsed." Reka plucked a shirt from the pile, held it up, and assessed the frayed edging.

"I've heard. I also heard she saved the lady from a wolf."

"Killed it with a curse and then murdered a Báthory guard."

"No," Mirella breathed, pushing her needle through the cloth. A messy stitch, not that it mattered much, the well-worn garment would be torn up for scraps soon enough. Something about the witch bothered her, not how she looked, ugly for sure, not even the rumors Reka liked to pass on with her own special embellishments.

A look in the witch's eyes that upset Mirella, like a demon peering through a window of an old tower. She reminded herself that the woman had left, swallowed by the doorway.

Mirella's hands shook. "Who?"

Reka dropped a shirt into a rumpled heap on her lap. "You know the Báthory guard, the one with the lovely eyes? Was one of his friends, the man didn't even make it to Sárvár, died out there in the witch's woods."

"Oh," Mirella said, lamely.

The two went quiet.

"He does have lovely eyes," Reka said.

A laughed bubbled from Mirella, shaky but the sunshine already chased her dark ruminations away, those would come back later, when the night came.

Reka, ever happy to bring her friend to good humor,

rummaged through the pile. "Bet he's got a shirt in here somewhere," she laughed, pulling at a random linen. "Ah here, I bet it smells divine." She pulled it to her nose and took a deep breath theatrically. "Oh yes, divine as horsehair."

Mirella erupted into laughter and the sunshine warmed again.

PART II
THE OLD MAN AND HIS DANCING GIRLS

13

The late afternoon made Dorottya restless, as did the memory of Ficzkó's pity and she could only think of going where no one would watch her. Ilona would be angry, but she needed to wander among the things that she knew best. Passing the kitchen garden, she pushed out toward the woods, like a lost child going home. The old man and his dancing girls followed, intangibly reaching her with the shadows cast by the towers, albeit lethargic and lazy in their endeavor. Dorottya shrugged them off, focusing on the trunks and foliage ahead.

Green greeted her. Leaves whispered together, discussed their small world and what things they drank in the damp fertility of their roots. A carnage of their ancestors, cannibalized, along with the discarded bodies of countless animals. These woods were wealthy. So much death and life existing side-by-side made for good foraging and already she found what it had to offer. Bits of blackberry leaves and celandine made their way into her pouches. The latter she gathered carefully, as too much of its juices were harmful. She eagerly added samples of mushrooms found cropping against trunks and hidden beneath ground cover.

But the one herb she needed most eluded her. Perhaps it only grew in her native woods. She shook her head. Surely more grew in these woods, she simply had to look. Foraging was an act of patience. Like love, she thought.

Ficzkó can't be foraged, fool.

57

Why not? Weren't there stories of humans falling in love with beasts?

The women were all maids, the men beasts. You are only a beast in the eyes of men, never anything more.

Dorottya could wait for him. She could be patient.

Ficzkó would know, one day, he'd see her steadfast love for him. She'd become pretty for him. Berries to dye her lips, she'd grow alluring. She imagined for a moment, those eyes smiling at her, admiring her like a lover. "You are beautiful," he'd say and sigh into her long hair.

He called her Dory.

A fool, the only true title Dorottya could claim. How laughable she'd imagined herself as anything else. Looks of pity she owned and nothing more.

They'd have children.

Dorottya scraped bark from a hardy-looking buckthorn, adding it to her collection as the woods darkened. The sun would find the horizon and dip beneath soon enough and then it would be too dark and foraging impossible. The old man awakened, prodding his dancing girls for amusement. He called Dorottya too, for his jester to bring her hideousness to him. He promised to make her pretty, if only she would entertain him for a while longer.

—

The Lady Nádasdy had kept Erszébet at arm's length and as isolated from the household as possible. "Have you received any summons from the baroness?" Susanna asked once the Reverend Magyari departed. Susanna had written to Lord Báthory concerning the matter several times, but so far there had been no letters in response . . . until this morning.

"No," Erszébet said. "Not even an invitation to dine. I have, however, been informed that my retinue has been dismissed." The girl's eyes glittered obsidian and unforgiving.

"Dismissed? By who?"

"The baroness, of course." Erszébet's face fell, but under the surface something dark and blighted had begun to grow.

"I've received no such word," Susanna said, confusion clouding her thoughts.

"You and your brother seem to be all that's left to me."

The nurse pursed her lips. "The witch too?"

Erszébet brooded. "No, she has apparently gone unnoted by the baroness."

Disappointing. At least the woman kept far from Erszébet's daily interactions. Susanna pulled a letter from her skirts. "Perhaps this will cheer you up."

"What is it?" The girl asked with apprehensive hope.

"A letter from your father arrived this morning. I wanted so much to give it to you but I thought it best if the pastor was not present."

The girl eagerly broke the wax seal, pulling at the parchment with barely contained excitement. Her glow peaked with flushed pride, but as her gaze made its way through the contents of the letter, she drooped.

A sharp pang went through Susanna's chest. "What did he say?"

"Nothing," Erszébet muttered. Disappointment pulled the flesh of her face, downward, just a touch. "Read it for yourself."

A formal greeting, telling, not that she expected affection from Lord Báthory, but distancing himself from his own child…

"He thinks I'm a monster," Erszébet said.

Expressions of the health of persons in the Báthory household, an accounting of dowry goods for shipment once the wedding were to occur, the birth of a foal—Erszébet had assessed accurately, the letter said nothing and by saying nothing it said something else entirely—"You are a mere pawn to advance the Báthory name. I owe you only formality, no more. I have gotten rid of you."

Memories of Erszébet, her hands smeared red, flooded Susanna. She shook her head. "Your lord father is probably afraid of the letter getting intercepted. I hear the countryside has gotten increasingly dangerous."

Erszébet's dark eyes regarded Susanna, and she could see herself reflected in them, a fly caught in amber. The girl didn't blink. The nurse felt heat rush to her cheeks, as if her thoughts had passed her lips and her fears were laid open for the girl to see. Maybe she'd see the love too. Dear God, let her see the love too. Silence roared in her ears.

The Nádasdy's had effectively put Erszébet on a mountain,

away and cloistered, turning even more pale from lack of fresh air and sunlight. Lord Báthory had left his daughter to her fate.

Erszébet admired herself in the hand mirror, lips pouted, her fingers wrapped around the legs of those dancing girls. Sometimes, Susanna couldn't tell where the mirror stopped and Erszébet began. Then, the girl let out an odd laugh, high and childlike. A chill raced up Susanna's spine.

"Yes, you are right about that. The countryside can be a dangerous." Erszébet's lips lost their color. She dropped the mirror on a table with a thud. "But so are caged dragons." She put a hand to her head, sitting down in a brocaded chair.

"Are you feeling ill?"

Dolefulness emanated from the girl, a sort of bleak humiliation. So far she'd been able to keep up appearances, and the illness that plagued her seemed to have been tamed. Erszébet peered from behind her hand. "The witch's medicine supply has run low and as of late . . . I've needed more and more to quell the headaches."

Susanna's stomach sank.

"I know," Erszébet said, acknowledging Susanna's unspoken thoughts. "But what other choice do I have?"

The nurse let out a long breath. "Shall I send for another batch?" Susanna regretted the words as soon as she had spoken them. Words of a coward.

"I have already sent your brother to visit her each day, but it seems the witch is rationing the tincture. The bottles I've received," Erszébet held one aloft to demonstrate, "have become less and less full."

"Why keep the witch here then?"

Erszébet shrugged. "I will find a use for her soon enough."

—

Dorottya dreamed that the old man was a devil and the girls, nymphs who rejoiced around him, naked as they drank from a cauldron of blood.

"Which one is the fairest?" they asked.

"Pick me," each exclaimed in turn.

He wheezed with delight and turned to Dorottya. "Which one?" He asked. "Who would you choose?"

14

First, tell them they are more special than the others.

Among them, do it again.

"Do you know who the first girl was?" He looks up from his book, the quill drooping in his hand.

"Oh, yes."

He expects a name. Again he thinks he's in control of all of this. No single person is in control without others. But a mass of them, a group together or simply supporting one person . . .

"She was young and pretty and happy."

Mostly, anyhow.

—

The book Susanna had found still swirled in her mind, as if it could see her from its perch in the other room. She suppressed a shiver despite the warmth of the day's intrusion on the stone walls. She wanted to go back to the room, to find that book and look again.

To be sure she hadn't dreamed it.

To look upon the devil.

Susanna chastised herself. Nothing in that room could calm her troubled thoughts. In fact, the whole castle only made things worse. She needed to move on and find her life. What did it all

61

mean without her child? Images of infant faces, her own son and Erszébet vied for attention in her heart. She'd have to let her son go, finally, and then when Erszébet married and became a baroness in her own right, Susanna would have to let her girl go too. Time to find her own way. Finally. If she had the strength to do it.

Ficzkó. For three nights she'd refused him. He'd be back tonight and the night after that, into eternity. Long ago, when she had tried to push him away, he'd chased her all the more until she couldn't stand it.

"Without me you are alone and lost. It's always been like that, we are meant to travel life together, dear sister," he'd said. His hands burned against her flesh.

The silence of her room pushed back at her and echoed against the stone and wood as if she dwelled in a hollowed-out giant. Never enough to fill the place and make it home. She couldn't help but wonder if Ficzkó told the truth, that without him, Susanna lost her way.

She tried to embroider but her fingers stiffened at the memory of the chamberlain's daughter, puffed and unrecognizable in her dress. Run away, a small voice inside her urged. Should have done that long ago.

Why had she come?

High above, the clouds curled in a languid dance against the blue sky. Below, the town of Sárvár lay beyond the castle walls, mere steps away from the causeway. From here, the outside world squirmed away all the while. She yearned for it, dreamed for the chance to live a life of her own.

Before it was too late.

—

Ficzkó leaned his head against the door to his sister's chambers. A stab of jealousy twisted in his gut. Did Susanna think she could leave him, like she had tried before?

The emptiness of his sister became impossible after the child died. He had tried to comfort her the only way he knew how. He'd held her tight as she wept, for days, kissed the salt upon her lips. When she finally stopped weeping and lay like a dead thing, vacant and unmoving, he took her. Giving way to his lust for her, driving his need until he quenched his thirst upon her womb yet again, with the hope he could give her another child. Always him. Her brother, who saved her, took care of her. For so long she reached for him, and only him. Who did she think got her the job as a nursemaid? Who did she think arranged for them both to accompany the girl to Sárvár? Always at risk to himself, even now, passing what tidbits that nasty baroness wanted about Erszébet and her family. For Susanna, for the two of them, he did all of this. When the baroness had wanted to dismiss Susanna, he'd been the one who stopped it. Him.

Taken care of her since they'd been on their own, left in that hovel as children.

Such unkindness, to pay him in nothing.

His skin prickled with heat.

Damnit, he thought, this was due to him. Everything he'd done and he asked only this. He relished no one like her. She knew that.

Why? Why did she refuse him?

Tears of frustration welled.

Work waited for him, hitches to build and loads of grain to move, while Susanna lived in comfort. For him, it would always be the heavy and dirtiest work. No playing at being highborn for him.

He trudged along the corridor of the wing, a resentment building in the pit of his stomach, a black and sticky thing.

A door swung open down the hall and he almost ran into Erszébet, her small stature materializing from her chamber.

"Excuse me, my lady, apologies." He managed to feign good humor.

She turned, her features surprised at first, and then they took on another look, something almost sinister. Some animal instinct within urged him to flee. She had certainly done things, but he had strength on his side.

Her lips parted in invitation.

He knew when a woman lusted for him—but coming from Erszébet, a noble and barely an adult, the realization startled him momentarily, then an idea took root. His sister's charge, how she fretted over the girl, tried to shield the corrupt product of the Báthory name. How low that fruit suddenly hung.

The idea of violating a noblewoman, especially Erszébet

turned his body electric. He'd watched the girl grow into this rose, now suddenly an offering to him to pluck. Erszébet regarded him with a smirk that he found maddening, a deep ache filled his member. What Susanna refused, he'd give to Erszébet and defile the perfect flower his sister so ardently cherished.

"It seems," Erszébet began, "that I am dining alone." She threw a glance behind her into her chambers. "Won't you join me?"

15

Dorottya ducked into the stables when she caught sight of the guards, locking herself into manure and straw. The horses nickered but quieted quickly, accustomed to her visits, to the ghost of a woman who strode past them to find a far shadowy corner for her ministrations.

She'd escape their looks.

Escape them all.

Dorottya gathered herself on the floor and made herself small. She willed invisibility. God, her hands ached, the flesh raw and cracked from washing. The water stripped them of moisture, such an odd thing, for moisture to take moisture.

Horrid. Horrid to look upon.

Shut up, mother.

Ugly. Ugliest I've ever seen.

Stop it.

He won't want you. How could he? You're disgusting.

SHUT UP.

Out there they want beauty. Best stay—

"STOP IT!" Dorottya put a surprised hand to her mouth. The horses pounded their hooves and snorted. She took a deep breath and let the swirling collection of stable smells move into her chest, fill her up.

He calls me Dory.

No one answered except the soft scrape of hooves on the dirt floor.

She imagined Ficzkó's eyes again. This time, she remembered the look of concern. "I never see you anywhere in the castle that Ilona hasn't sent you," he had said. "Never at meals."

Stay here, she thought, and let mother be right. Dorottya pounded a fist into her thigh. No.

She had been the one who chose to leave the woods.

It would be mealtime soon. After fetching her portion from the kitchens, she'd go to the hall and eat with the other servants. Maybe Ficzkó would be there and she'd dine alongside him.

The horses nickered in approval.

Mother quieted. A glorious silence signaled Dorottya's victory. In her mind, she twirled with one of the dancing girls. Free, free, free.

Footsteps took her unawares. The stall door flung open. Guards, framed by the doorway, sneered at her. Beside them, a stable boy quivered.

"I thought you were stealing," the boy said, his eyes wide.

One of the guards began to laugh. "It's the fucking witch. No wonder the boy's so scared. She'd scare me in the shadows too."

The other guard took a step forward, the one who liked to kick mud. "I don't like witches." His face darkened into a cynical mask of violent possibilities. "I like ugly women even less."

"What has a witch ever done to you?" The moment the words left Dorottya's mouth she knew it had been a mistake. The mask broke and his raw hatred shined like the surface of new ink.

"Sold a charm to my brother to save him from fever." He paused. "Didn't save him from anything," he said, his voice low and dangerous.

The other guard spit.

"Charms don't always work," Dorottya said. Her voice came out limp and useless. The rage simmered far away inside of her. She couldn't make it hers, couldn't use it to save herself.

"Janos," the maid, Reka, called out in her girlish voice. Soft taps of jogging footsteps. "There you are. My lady has given me leave for supper." The maid stopped. her lashes waved like fans above each widened eye. "I'm—

"Don't you wish you were a real woman?" Janos pointed at the maid. "Like that."

Reka quieted and her face flushed.

"Does it hurt to be so ugly?" The first guard sneered.

"Well, does it?" Janos said. "Does it?"

The stable boy fled.

Where was Ficzkó now? As if the question would summon him to save her as he'd done before. This time though, her hands shook, she knew it would be worse and no one would save her.

Reka tried to feign amusement, as if they joked. "Come on, Janos. Leave the witch alone."

Dorottya padded backwards, straw crunching under her feet. Her back found the wall suddenly with a thud. "Yes," she said in response, her words low and desperate.

He leaped at her, grabbing cruelly at her breast, and tore the lacing of her bodice, leaving her chest exposed.

"You pig whore." Janos whirled, spittle flying. "Now that's a woman," he pointed to the maid. "Show her, Reka. Come on girl, half of us have seen them plenty anyway."

Both he and his friend laughed.

Reka's smile melted, she looked toward the doors.

"Do it," Janos said. His words tipped with promises of violence.

She jumped.

"Come on now."

Coloring, the maid moved mechanically, slowly undoing the laces. Tugging them slack, pushing away the fabric of the shift underneath. She turned her head as if, by not looking, she'd be less exposed.

"Now that there is a fine set," he said, staring at the maid's chest and pulling Dorottya's breast cruelly, his curled fingers nearly shredding flesh.

Dorottya let out a cry, fear and pain giving way to a gargle of hopelessness.

"The teets of a witch, this is what suckling the devil does."

Ugly. Ugliest I've ever seen.

He spit in Dorottya's face.

———

Dorottya stumbled from the stables, a hand still at her bodice, trying to keep the pieces of herself from falling apart. Blood ran over her face. Servants turned to her as she passed. They, with their pretty lips and wide eyes, made for kissing, made for showing. Kiss them, push out the entrails and heart, crack open the ribs like a door and fall deep asleep inside.

They stared. All the ones with perfect ankles, bones as fine as birds, crackling in her teeth. The rags of Dorottya's dress rustled like regalia, she danced with the girls. They all wished they could crawl into each other. Layers of people and flesh.

She twirled.

The guard had danced with her, danced like she was a pig. How did he dance with the maid? Did he make her a pig too?

"Don't forget how we treat witches." His fingers had dug into her arms, purple sleeves, swelling, decorated with touch.

"Oink, oink," she said.

Pretty statues and breasts like jeweled earrings.

Strands of silk and ribbon falling from their heads.

Falling heads.

The cold flesh of dancing girls beneath her feet.

The old man stared back at her. He squatted, fingers held out, he cupped her face, licking her with his forked tongue. Barbed feet tapped the ground.

He tasted like mud.

Like sweet slop and rotten vegetables.

16

"I've been promoted," Ficzkó said. Susanna watched her brother quietly. They hadn't talked since his last visit to her chambers, neither had he returned. Not all what she expected, yet he managed to appear frequently, as if he'd been there all along. Waiting in the shadow for a summons.

Erszébet arched an eyebrow. "I don't recall doing that."

Two maids scurried past, carrying loads. Autumn arrived, painting even the sky with its colors. She had heard reports that this winter would be a harsh one. A maid threw a glance at Ficzkó under her lashes. Susanna buzzed with irritation and immediately chided herself.

Cobbles formed swirling designs under their feet and overhead arches framed the edges of the courtyard.

"Lady Nádasdy has seen it fit to meld their household and yours together as a show of unity."

Erszébet stopped. "My household? You, Susanna and my horse? The Nádasdy numbers swell with our addition, I see."

"My lady, I am your loyal servant of heart."

"I don't see how she would think to have any authority to do such a thing."

"Authority, my lady, has much to do with capability. And the truth is that your influence is limited here in Sárvár. You are hidden, with few in the household who would speak for you."

Ficzkó threw a glance to Susanna, a silent plea for support.

Erszébet's face twisted darkly. "How can I? Lady Nádasdy keeps me cloistered like a nun. I've yet to even see the countryside that I will become baroness over. How do you suppose I can manage something I've never seen? Or ensure the safety of the serfs I'm bound to protect?" Erszébet stopped. "Peasants want and need a noble to love. I intend to be just that. Holding love and fear in equal measure is how you maintain loyalty."

The sun made its final yawn and a few servants had begun to hang lanterns. The same girl passed again. Ficzkó glanced at her. Did Susanna see a slight change, a softening of his features? Perhaps a trick of the light? And why on earth did she care?

"I have another surprise," Ficzkó said. "The outcome of a well laid plan."

"You've arranged to become the next Lord Nádasdy?" Erszébet said with a light laugh, it sounded odd echoing off the cobblestones.

"No, my lady, I'll leave that to you." Ficzkó shifted. "I've convinced Lady Nádasdy to allow an excursion to the surrounding Nádasdy lands."

Susanna clapped her hands together. "Truly?"

"You leave in the morning with a few Nádasdy guards, if you are willing, my lady." He finished with a flourish and a bow.

Annoyance melted from Erszébet. "How did you manage?"

"I have a way with noble women," he said with a mischievous grin that set off bells in Susanna's head.

"Indeed, you do." Erszébet extended a hand for Ficzkó to kiss. "Yes. I would like that very much."

—

Both Erszébet and Susanna rose in the dark morning hours because of their excitement. They felt like girls, whispering as they lit candles, donning the riding gowns Susanna had set out the night before. Erszébet stubbed her toe on a chest, which sent them both into fits of stifled laughter. Susanna wanted to grab ahold of the threads of this morning and never let them go.

She bound Erszébet's hair, off the proud and high Báthory brow and produced a stash of fresh berries to stain their lips.

When the first drizzle of sunshine pushed over the horizon, they clasped fingers and rushed out the door, leaving the guards confused. The pair regained their composure as they neared the courtyard, tugging at their bodices and smoothing their hair. Susanna pushed open the door with a nod. Two guards had made a carriage emblazoned with the Nádasdy crest ready for their departure.

Erzsébet pursed her lips and strode ahead. "I wish to ride."

The guard's unfurled hand dropped sharply as he rose from a bow. "My lady, I don't recommend—

"I cannot see clearly from a Nádasdy carriage. The very crest seems to come with a cloister. I will be protector over these lands, over the wives and daughters of the Nádasdy household and the household of the lands overseen by the Nádasdy name. I will be seen. I will taste the air of the land and smell the harvest. So please, sirs, honor my request, and allow me to ride so that one day, I can justly act in the interest of our people."

The guards had turned to listen. One of them, a lean scrap of a man with long gray hair, turned to a boy and pointed to the stable. The child scurried away quickly.

Susanna let out a breath she didn't realize she had been holding and stood a little straighter behind her charge.

The guard inclined his head, his lips curving. "As you say, my lady."

A boy led a midnight charger, a magnificent steed, the kind that needed a skilled hand to rule its restless disposition. Not unlike Erzsébet herself. Likely, the Nádasdy guard tested the girl, bringing out such a robust animal. But Écsed was in the countryside, often with little to do than go riding, and Erzsébet had spent many hours in the saddle with much less cooperative steeds.

Once saddled, Erzsébet approached the animal slowly and confidently, talking in soft tones to the steed, allowing it get the scent of her. It nickered once, and fell into the girl's hands as she reached for it, and mounted the saddle before anyone had time to offer assistance.

The lean guard let out a hoot of appreciative laughter. "Now then, there's the kind of mistress I want protecting my wifie." He gave a sudden bashful glance at Erzsébet and cleared his throat. "Begging your pardon, my lady."

A shadow passed in a window above and Susanna recognized the silhouette of the baroness, who withdrew into the shadows of the chamber. Always in watchful control, that woman. She'd succeeded so far in controlling Erszébet, but Susanna doubted that the woman knew what type of creature she confronted.

Elena's bashed face haunted her.

You know, Susanna thought to herself, don't you?

Blood, dried beneath her charge's fingernails, the scratch of Greek letters against parchment.

"Our ancestors were born with six legs." Erszébet pulled away the careful coif Susanna had set earlier, chestnut hair tumbled in long waves like a Báthory banner.

Susanna looked away.

This place gave no grace.

The entourage moved toward the gate where the land shined like heaven itself. Susanna dallied behind. For a moment, she watched the bigger players in a bigger world than hers. She'd fade away. She'd been fading for so long. Once Erszébet no longer needed her, she'd be forgotten completely. Would she melt into the shadows? No one would speak her name. Worse, no one would be left to speak her son's name.

"Elek," she said. Her soft breath came out in a mist, as if his name took material form. She could still feel the weight of his tiny body in her arms.

Susanna bowed her head, urging her mare forward, and she passed out the gate.

17

The lady had left.

Along with her, Dorottya had given her last bottle. A thousand straps seemed to tighten around her innards. What could she do? If she could not provide this one thing, the lady would surely send her away.

Away from her. My lady, lady, lady, lady . . .

It hurt, guards holding her down, shredding her skin. Booted feet kicking.

Ugly. Ugliest I've ever seen.

She hummed. The devil had pretty words. Pretty like my lady. A goddess. Queen of women.

Must find the flower. She lined tiny bottles along the table, like little soldiers and winced.

Her head hurt, a flash, a blinding light of pain. Dorottya grit her teeth.

Fire.

She'd have that.

18

The countryside bustled in the throes of the final harvest. Bales stacked along the edges of fields. Field workers plucked root vegetables from their earthy beds. Most folks were streaked with dirt, huffing in the chill air.

"It's a good harvest, my lady," said a ruddy farmer.

"Show me, sir. I'd love to see the wealth of the land." Erszébet dismounted, pulling up her skirts to step over a manure pile. The old guard chuckled.

The farmer beamed, then a hasty doubt moved over his features. "It's a humble place, my lady."

Erszébet placed a hand on his arm. "There is no need for shame, you have much to be proud of."

Tears misted the farmer's eyes. "Thank you, my lady. Lord Nádasdy has a treasure in you. I have the apple harvest, I'm particularly proud, the best in all of Hungary."

As she watched Erszébet win over the peasants, Susanna's breast swelled again with pride. The farmer led them into an outbuilding. Cold light poured in from a multitude of cracks. Over the packed earth floor stood barrels and barrels of apples. Pink ones in full blush, bright scarlets that promised a heady sweetness and ones whose skin were stained such a red they appeared daringly black. Both Erszébet and Susanna gasped with delight.

"Pick one, my Lady, try it," the farmer said, holding a welcoming arm out. "And for your folk too, there is plenty."

Erszébet examined the barrels, assessing each, feeling the flesh with deft fingers, and finally settled on one of the darkest reds. The farmer puffed up with pride and nodded at her, urging a taste.

Erszébet brought the apple to her lips and with flash of white teeth she bit down, eyes fluttering closed, chewing and savoring. "I don't think I've tasted anything so delicious. What are they called?"

The farmer glowed. "I call them Midnight Ladies. A special hybrid I've developed over many years. Finally perfected."

"Well sir, I will require you to send me regular shipments of your harvest. I must have them in the castle. I will take three barrels immediately."

The farmer bowed, blubbering his joy. "You'll always get the best, my lady, the best."

"Have the barrels loaded and the give the man payment for his superb cultivation," Erszébet directed.

"They love you," Susanna whispered, as they headed back to the horses.

"I love them too," Erszébet said. "I suppose it makes sense. I've always been closer to the low born. You probably shouldn't tell my father." She laughed.

Susanna's chest hummed, feeling like the love for Erszébet would burst her open. She reached out and placed a hand upon the daughter of her heart. Erszébet smiled, eyes sparkling, and she squeezed Susanna's hand in return.

The group turned back toward town. Along the way, commoners working the field waved and ran breathless toward the Nádasdy bannermen. Word had traveled quickly.

"For my lady," they would say, before passing along bit of their harvest, pieces of their handiwork—a scrap of embroidery, a carved figure in the shape of a folk woman, a colorful shawl. The welcome that had been denied Erszébet now met her tenfold. She bloomed, her hair tumbling in the breeze.

The lady of the people.

—

A gloom cast over them both as soon as their horses hit the cobbles of Sárvár town. The castle loomed and watched with wide unblinking eyes, as if the baroness's sight could pierce the town to find them. When an innkeeper beseeched Erszébet to come dine, the girl eagerly accepted, slowing their inevitable return.

"It will be dark shortly," Susanna said. "Ladies do not stay out after dark, especially high-born ones."

"There are lanterns and we are so close," Erszébet said. "Come, we could use a good meal."

"Be careful, Erszébet," Susanna warned. "The baroness will not be pleased."

"I'll pay the price for it later. I don't want to go back to my prison yet." The girl's face tightened. "Come, let's enjoy ourselves for a while longer."

The innkeeper cleared a large room, filling it with glasses of wine. Food poured in from the inn's kitchens—loaves of crusty bread, piles of fresh butter and bowls of fisherman's stew brimming with fresh fish from the river. A young woman arrived with a flute, telling stories with the dance of notes as she played, singing of happiness and sorrow, victory and loss.

The room grew cozy with music and full bellies, yet Susanna fretted.

"She is wonderful!" Erszébet exclaimed, clapping her hands together.

The innkeeper bowed. "Thank you, my lady. My daughter has more talent in her little finger than I have in my whole body." He laughed.

Susanna murmured as the sky faded from crimson to black, "My lady, we should return."

"Yes, yes," Erszébet replied dismissively, drinking deep from her wine cup.

Susanna wanted to drag her back. But back to what? A highborn prison, she thought, one she condemned herself to as well.

Susanna stepped into the main room. News of the Nádasdy's betrothed must have spread and the inn filled with patrons. Mostly men, their hats wrinkled in fists, fatigue drawing lines around eyes. Even the younger men were not immune. One of them stared hard at her, making her itch.

The room spun.

She needed air.

Susanna rushed into the street and sucked in the cool night. A wind rushed between the buildings and shoved its fingers into her bones. Even the layers of her riding dress could not shield her. But she needed to feel wind's promise of winter's brutal cold, needed to strip herself of this life. How though? Where would she go? And Ficzkó, what would she do about him? She owed him so much it made her chest ache.

A chill gust tingled Susanna but she refused to shield herself. Let the cold take her. Let Erszébet find her in the morning right here, a frozen dead woman. Wasn't she that already?

A dark shape stirred in the shadows. The devil heard her. He'd descended from the castle to collect her soul and she deserved every flame that waited for her in Hell. The shape inched forward. The shadow's tentacles reached for her.

She leaned toward it, welcoming the end.

Shadow's edges sharpened and creeped closer to lantern light. Soon, Susanna could make out an outline of a figure and a haggard old woman's face. A tide of wrinkles pulled at the corners of a mouth that had long ago swallowed its own lips. Her eyes were strong, wide, and empty of lashes.

"What do you want?" Susanna choked.

The old woman only gaped.

Susanna's breath seared the air, moving into the old woman's slack mouth, giving it life, fusing it with sounds it longed so much to speak.

"I didn't know the watcher knew me. But it knows, it knows and made me perfect. In the white of the snow, I lay, my blood like garnets on the winter," the old woman said.

"I don't understand." The cold air no longer welcomed Susanna and she wished desperately to turn the latch behind her and rush back into the room she had run from moments ago. She wished for Ficzkó.

"Run." The old woman licked her lips. "Run away, away from the devil."

A warm hand closed around her own, gripping her tightly. Susanna yelped in surprise.

"That's enough Néni," said a man.

"I see the watcher."

"Get home," he barked.

The old woman's eyes went vacant. She bobbed her head in agreement as if the man had given her a wonderful idea.

Susanna's heart bounced inside her chest wildly.

The man pulled Susanna gently toward the door. "Come inside," he said.

Too shaken to object, she did as he bid.

The door shut behind them, the heavy wood shuttering and then going still like a wall, a blessed, blessed wall. Now the heat and sounds of jovial voices brought comfort. Just a senile old woman, Susanna thought, nothing more. Her hands shook and she stumbled. The man steadied her. Just as tired as the others, his mouth set into frown as he offered her a chair.

"You alright?" he said.

Susanna put a hand to her head. Was she alright? She had no idea. "Thank you," she said.

He nodded. "Been awhile since I've seen her."

"Who?"

"Néni." His mustache twitched and he scratched at the wiry hairs on his chin that passed as a beard. "She hasn't been well, age and a big imagination."

The music stopped. The fiddler and singer sipped drinks. Susanna glanced around, terrified that she'd see the face of the old woman. "Poor woman," Susanna said, taking a shuddered breath.

The man patted her hand and called for drinks.

"Néni's mind addled right around the heavy snow last winter. Do you remember it?"

"No," Susanna took a sip of the wine, "We haven't been at the castle long enough to see a winter yet."

"We?" He asked and seemed to look at Susanna's gown for the first time, "You mean the noble, you're with her?" He gestured to the busy adjacent room, his eyes widened. "Forgive me, my lady, I didn't realize."

"Please, I am not highborn, I simply serve the lady." Susanna glanced at the room with guilt. "I should get back."

He nodded and issued a cough.

"I'm her nurse," Susanna explained, tucking hair behind an ear.

"Yes." He flashed a snaggle-toothed smile. "Name is Agoston." He thrust out a hand.

She took it. "Susanna," she said. "Thank you for the wine. I have coin."

"Nah," he said, and glanced away. "Bought it for a reason."

"I"—Susanna's ear-tips burned—"I appreciate the kindness." Right now, she didn't want solitude, even less, alone in a room full of people, or alone next to Erszébet.

The inn's common room warmed. Agoston relaxed. He told her about his woodworking shop and snippets of information about the woman, Néni.

"Does she have someone to look after her?" Susanna asked.

Agoston finished a swig and wiped his mouth on a sleeve. "Her daughter. Could do a better job of it."

Susanna shook her head. "Sad."

"It is, but no one is willing to take on the job. How about you?" His lips twisted wryly.

She almost choked and then managed a small laugh. "No, no. I have enough to take care of with my charge."

The room had thinned of patrons, only a few left in the corners, a man dozed in his seat. Night wrapped around the inn heavily and Susanna realized she had been gone for some time. Much too long.

"I'm so sorry, Agoston," Susanna noted the nearby room had fallen quiet and dark. "I must go. I'm overdue to attend my lady."

He searched her face. "You aren't happy to go."

She smiled as she stood. "I wish I could stay right here and talk with you." Admitting it ached. Foolish, like a young girl flirting with a crush.

"If you need anything, Susanna, my shop is further down a ways there." He pointed and said, "Come find me."

Something about his offer made her feel safe, a kindness she did not deserve. For a moment, she considered embracing the man. Instead, she inclined her head. "Thank you, Agoston. I am very lucky to have met you tonight."

———

"My lady's gone to her room," one of the guards explained. Susanna recognized the older one from the courtyard. He reclined comfortably with a few others, a full tankard of wine on the table.

"Room?"

Another guard cleared his throat. "My lady thought it best to stay here for the night."

How long had Susanna been gone?

"It is late," the guard offered, as if reading her thoughts. "Probably best not to have someone of her status out in the night. Never know who you'll meet."

Indeed.

Maybe a kind gentleman.

Or a frightening old woman.

"Thank you, sirs." Susanna shivered before rushing up the wooden stairs. As she expected, she easily found which room Erszébet had taken. Set aside with a private entrance. The flute girl curled in a corner beside the door, her chin bouncing from her chest as she startled herself awake.

"No, no, it is alright," Susanna said, stopping the girl from rising. "Is the lady inside?"

"Yes madam," the girl said.

The shiver returned. Susanna thought of the devil, his tongue reaching for her. The old woman had been warning her, but about what? Did Néni know something? Susanna couldn't help but feel the warning had something to do with the book she found in the abandoned castle room. But how could Néni know of the book? It made no sense.

"Run," the old woman had said.

Too many memories danced behind her eyes. The flute girl frowned at her as if she saw them too.

Run.

Susanna would make a plan soon.

Honor her pledge to Lord Báthory to see Erszébet to the wedding, she'd ensure the girl remained chaste, a simply enough task. Chaste? Susanna hadn't even been there to watch her tonight. Instead she'd gone off and had a drink with a man she didn't even know.

Susanna pushed the door open, sure she'd find her charge in the throes of sin. The fire in the hearth had burned to embers, its faint glow the only source of light. Rich velvet darkness covered all else like a blanket.

"My lady?" she whispered.

A candle flared to life and Susanna's heart turned to lead in her chest. Propped in a chair, Erszébet sat enthroned, the candle flame casting a flicking light across her features, turning them haunted and grim.

"It's gone," Erszébet said. An empty bottle dropped to the floor with a muffled clatter. "I need more."

Susanna inhaled deeply.

"I need it, so I can be everything they want me to be." A child's voice, small and lost.

"What if you didn't? What if"—daring overcame Susanna—"we left, escaped, went on our own into the countryside, away from here and all the things others want?" Her hands shook. "What if we escaped and lived like a normal mother and daughter?"

Erszébet's strange eyes glittered obsidian. "You don't understand."

"I understand enough to see this place isn't good for you. Being a noble and all the expectations, it isn't fair, Erszébet, you should be a child without cares. At least once." Hot with rebellion, a stab of determination went through Susanna's middle. Daring to hope. "It doesn't have be this way."

"No. That's not it." The girl went still, too still. "We can't leave. Nobility swallows you up before you're even awake to know it. Then you become part of the web. We are just as much part of that web as the spider, we spin the threads over the same structure and it becomes us too. After that, it is all survival."

Susanna's wish became fervent, finally spoken out loud, finally admitted it to herself. "Please, my daughter, my girl. Please. You can become part of something else that gives you life and joy."

"No," Erszébet seethed. "This gives me joy."

Susanna fell silent.

"I am not your daughter." Erszébet slumped from the chair, her small body convulsing into odd lines and angles made more grotesque by the shadows. Susanna rushed to her side, pulling the girl to her as she always did, holding her close as the fit shook every inch of her child and vomit oozed from her mouth.

19

The sun reddened the sky and a chill creeped into the air and into Mirella. Their duties were done for the day, unless of course, Ilona called them for some urgent Nádasdy demand. But for now, she had a moment of freedom and she had been able to save an extra sweet for Reka and her to share.

Reka must have finished early, since she was no longer mending or fetching water. Mirella went to look for her friend in the hall where they sometimes slept when the weather grew chilly. A few servants already huddled within, staking claim to the coveted spots by the hearth. In the winter, fights would break out over who got to sleep the closest to the fire. Reka always gave up her spot to the children and older servants. But she was not there now. Sometimes, Reka could be found along the west wall, or checking on the youths who worked the stables. Yet no one had seen her there either.

When the sun had all but set, Mirella rested against the darkened wall. She pulled the sweet from her pocket, giving up the idea of sharing, and took a honey-apple filled bite. The blasted thing tempted her to gobble it all down, but guilt moved her to rewrap it. She might find Reka yet. Perhaps she had duties in another part of the castle. Undoubtedly, she'd end up in the hall like most of the servants. As Mirella pushed off the wall, a hand clapped over her mouth, a hot breath buried itself in her hair, sniffing like an animal.

The pastry dropped to the ground.

Mirella tried to scream.

"I've been watching you, Mirella," said a familiar voice. "And waiting. Finally it is time. I've come to make you what you were always meant to be."

20

"Were there accomplices? People who assisted?"
"You haven't been listening."

—

Shrieks—raw pulses of energy that bounded through the air and bounced from stonewall slabs to cold floors. Dorottya trembled, soiled linens dropped from suddenly slack hands. The other maids pushed at their head scarves, their dainty brows furrowed in confusion. Full lips asking, moving, without sound.

Make me perfect—

It came again, high and shrill, rushing from the courtyard, pulling at her, urgent. Somewhere, another Dorottya answered, insisted she do something, making her move and yank urgently at the old wood door into the courtyard. Stuck, the wood swelled with the ever-present moisture of the bathhouse.

More screams, gruff voices tense with fear.

A sob.

Dorottya's heart thudded and she threw herself backward with a fierce tug, hitting her back against a wall in the process, blood bloomed in her mouth, tasting no different than tears and sweat. Chill air rushed in and Dorottya hurried out.

Ilona pushed aside a screaming girl. The older woman

84

hunched to the ground, busy, working. Dorottya moved to her instinctively, past a stable hand and guard.

Ficzkó panted, laying on the courtyard cobbles, his arm bent oddly and quickly turning into what looked like a swollen bag of broken teeth. The spoked wheels of a carriage, blazoned with the Nádasdy crest, had been pushed away. Ilona looked up, her lips moved and murmured comforting sounds over Ficzkó. A maid ran off, perhaps to fetch help, or out of horror. The men stood dumbfounded. At least the guard threw a question at Ilona, "What can I do?"

"Move him to the washroom," Dorottya said. She glanced at Ilona, "I believe you have use for a healer now."

"Yes." The gruff older woman's voice came out in a rush.

"I can treat him better there." Dorottya put a hand on her friend's brow. "Ficzkó," she whispered in his ear, "you believed in this forest witch before, believe for a little longer."

His colorless lips spoke of endless pain that made her heart twist.

Ilona shouldered Ficzkó's weight along with the guard, her stocky frame bearing the weight with little hardship. They bustled Ficzkó into the washroom, laying the man down on a pile of freshly dried linen. He was limp.

"A fire," Dorottya ordered. Ilona moved without question and threw fresh logs into the ashes. The witch leveled a gaze at the guard. "A bit of rope, a good thick stick, and an axe."

Dorottya didn't bother to look to see that the man had gone, she ran for her quarters on her own mission to fetch pouches of dried herbs, bottles and needles.

She returned well before the guard and quickly got to work. They would have to do this rapidly before the swelling made removal imprecise. She shoved a rolled cloth containing birch bark and other herbs between Ficzkó's teeth. She hoped to save his tongue, once they began to cut. If he was lucky, he would stay unconscious, far enough away in his dreams to survive what she must do. Sometimes, pain alone could kill.

The guard returned. He breathed hard, his chest expanding and contracting in rapid movements. Dorottya looped the rope onto the upper arm, the part still identifiable as human. The rest of the arm moved, jelly-like, and had broken open in some parts, seeping gore onto the linens. She tightened the rope with the stick, creating a winch. Each moment, twisting further and further, until the rope became impossibly tight, pushing away the unhealthy parts of the arm like sausage spilled from its casing.

Ficzkó groaned, but did not wake.

"The fire is ready," Ilona said.

Dorottya nodded and lifted the axe into the guard's hands. "Is your aim good?"

"I—

"It best be."

—

It had taken two hacks of the ax for the guard to sever what was left of Ficzkó's arm. The man had woken wild and screaming, Ilona held him down. The heated pot used to sear flesh and staunch bleeding silenced him again into unconsciousness. Now came the slow watch. Once a patient survived amputation, a new battle awaited.

Dorottya cleaned the linens and lay down beside him in exhaustion. Before long, she gave way to sleep. The devil waited in her dreams.

He caressed and enfolded her with leathery wings. He summoned the dancing girls who twirled in their pretty country dresses, their blood feeding the soil of the great castle. Dorottya followed the veiny roots branching beneath, pushing through earth and into the forest beyond.

She woke startled by Ficzkó's moan of agony. Ilona had hung linens about them, a rudimentary gesture of respect. Dorottya checked for signs of fever but found none. Instead of relief, she nursed the pit of knowledge of these things. There would many more checks and many more possibilities for fever to poison him.

Work bustled beyond the make-shift linen walls, but Dorottya saw only Ficzkó, his rough cheekbones, half-bent nose and sparse chin hair. Where he would have been described as wiry and strong yesterday, within mere hours looked gaunt and sallow.

Dorottya thought about Susanna, gone with their ladyship to visit the surrounding countryside. How long would it take for news to reach them?

Ugly.

Ficzkó groaned, and then rasped.

Dorottya moved to his side.

"Susanna?" He whispered in a way that filled Dorottya's eyes with tears. Not for Ficzkó and his sister, but for herself.

"No," she said. "It's Dory."

His eyelids fluttered and he fell quiet again. His lips looked bruised and painful. Dorottya put a hand on his cheek and the fierce heat startled her.

Fever.

Tension mounted in her shoulders.

As she feared, the battle for his life had only just begun.

21

"Am I pretty yet? Isn't there a bawdy lyric someplace—No riches are needed when breasts of sweetest fruit that you bear, Oh, lovely is she, who kills in her sleep and not one of the lawmen did care."

The interrogator has his hands folded. He seems vexed.

"Are you a married man?" The rhyming has stuck. Man, than, Anne.

Someone is laughing.

Anne, like the prostitute in town.

Perfect.

Make me perfect.

—

Riding out into the damp morning toward the castle was the same as being underwater. Susanna wanted to thrash against it, but she knew the more she struggled, the more she'd likely drown. Somewhere deep inside of her, she knew the drowning would come, but if she cooperated, pretended she didn't know or notice, kept quiet, she could delay it, maybe even find that one moment to escape. Her fingers wandered to the tiny wooden cross in her pocket. Agoston had run through an alleyway with it, offering it to her without words but with his flushed face full with emotion. The long causeway that marked the entrance to the castle loomed just ahead, and Susanna longed to return to town.

The guards leaned back into their saddles, eyes still half-lidded with sleep. As they passed under the portcullis, a scruffily-dressed servant jogged out to meet them. Erszébet brought her horse round, pulling on the reigns with dainty hands.

"My lady," the servant called. His voice shook when he spoke. "I have news."

"Speak it, then." Erszébet didn't move her head, only her eyes, her stare ran hard and straight along the bridge of her nose, piercing the manservant. He paused and gulped. Something about the girl had grown powerful. Perhaps Lady Nádasdy had been wise to limit her future daughter-in-law's movements.

The servant bowed. "There's been an accident with one of your men."

"I still have men?" Erszébet answered, throwing a glance at the Nádasdy soldiers that had accompanied them. The older man inclined his head. "Who is it then?"

"The man they call Ficzkó."

Blood drained from Susanna's face and settled into a knot in her stomach. Stepping forward involuntarily, dreading the worst, she balled her fingers into her skirts. "Is he alive?"

"Yes, madam, but badly hurt."

"What has happened?" Erszébet asked, her speech turning hushed and childlike, she put a hand on her nurse's shoulder. The girl's palm radiated heat through the cloth.

"My lady . . . a carriage crushed his arm, it's been severed." The man paused, his mouth still open.

Fear crawled up Susanna's throat. "Where is he?"

"With the witch."

A soft sniffle came from Erszébet who ran a sleeve across her eyes. "Go," Erszébet said. "Go look after your brother."

Susanna held her body painfully still.

"I'll be alright," Erszébet said. Her grip on Susanna's shoulder tightened in contrast to her words. The nurse shook free of this girl-who-was-not-her-daughter and pulled away and rushed wordlessly toward the washroom.

22

Her brother lay on a bed of old aprons and linens, his features deflated and ghostly. Susanna paused, her stomach tightening into a ball.

The witch leaned beside Ficzkó. She pushed his dark hair away from his unresponsive face, her touch tender . . . loving. The cross in Susanna's pocket suddenly grew heavy and shameful.

"Hello," Susanna said, trying to soften her voice but the woman jumped just the same. "I'm sorry"—nothing but a neatly packed stump where Ficzkó's right arm had been.

The witch's lips tightened as she followed Susanna's gaze. "Just finished redressing it."

"I didn't know." Susanna's chin trembled, trying to shake the tears loose. She held on, wanting to be strong. Ficzkó always said she didn't know about strength, but he'd never nursed a child and put that child in a grave.

Beyond the cloth, maids bustled in their chores and Ilona's curt voice issued commands and complaints.

"What will happen?" Susanna asked, afraid of the answer.

The witch's face pinched. "Don't know. He's full with fever."

"I"—Susanna noted the dark circles on the witch's face, deep lines of sleeplessness and anguish. Her heart softened despite her suspicions. Maybe she had misjudged this woman.

Susanna moved to Ficzkó. "I will stay with him so you can rest."

"Rest?" said Dorottya, swallowing hard, a strange wild light in her eyes. "No. Need to brew more medicine. Follow the roots and pluck them." Her lips spotted with spittle.

Susanna stiffened, trying to stop the revulsion from showing. "I understand," Susanna said as the witch moved to leave. No, not witch, what was it that Ficzkó called the woman? "Dory," she called.

The woman turned, that wild look grew and glinted like a blade.

"Thank you," Susanna said.

—

Dorottya eyed the woods with exhausted desperation. She needed more to treat Ficzkó, but also needed to search again for some sign of herbs for her ladyship's tincture, or at least a temporary alternative. She walked down the hill, off the path, and cast herself into the darkness of the foliage. No peace found her. Instead, her stomach churned as she passed through the patterns of black and green. Ever since the stables, she had been swimming in a river, forever surging and moving her with its will. The old man, always waking, he called to be entertained. The girls dancing in circles so constant and dizzying that Dorottya begged them to stop.

She wandered, listless, dropping what little she found into her gathered apron.

Ficzkó needed her. She shouldn't be away for long.

A large fallen tree, mostly hollowed by rot and moisture, lay a short distance ahead. Secret nooks where mushrooms liked to grow, peeking like shy maidens who hid their lust behind veneers of modesty. They all wanted worship.

Pale shapes drew her, but as she neared, the mushrooms became something else. As the shape of a foot collected in her consciousness, Dorottya's breath caught in her throat. The trees bent their canopy as if hiding their treasure, jealous that a mere mortal like her would discover it. In a trance, a bubble of excitement drove her. The old man couldn't see her this far, could he?

He'd want treasure too.

The hollow of the tree pointed upwards, displaying its wares toward the trees alone. She'd have to scramble over several adjoining logs to get a look inside. Balancing on their slick, moss covered surfaces, Dorottya managed to pull herself to the edge.

The foot became a leg, this giving way to the full the shape of a young woman. Bereft of a frock, the woman's small breasts budded, her hips curving an invitation to admirers. So pale, her flesh, it looked as if a collection of snow dusted her, daring to touch the perfection with its icy fingers. Someone had decorated her. Lips puckered with fresh flowers, thin Thornberry branches woven into her blonde hair, apple blooms huddled over the pelvis, conspiring to keep something for themselves.

Her stomach turned to ice. She knew this girl, recognized her. She was one of the washing maids, the prettiest one, Mirella. Dorottya sneered. The one who'd flash her ankles every time Ficzkó came to call, one of the whisperers, all goggling eyes and muffled insults. A gorge of hate filled Dorottya's throat and then satisfaction. The maid lay here now, in this state, conquered and lifeless. She'd rot soon. Dorottya thought about how that pretty face would look eaten by worms.

23

"Do you think all of this could have happened if Hungary was at peace? Do you think there would be less bloodshed and suffering?"

He's uncomfortable with questions. They make him think about other things when he should be thinking about guilt and punishment.

"Nobles bled the common folk dry, long before these girls bled."

He writes in his book, his nose so close to the page that it might get ink on it. "So you admit that these girls were bled?"

Closed again, not listening, not hearing.

"It never had to do with the blood. It was about the absence, the cleanliness of the vessel left behind."

———

November, 1573

Ferenc returned home the moment he received the summons to join the Habsburg military effort against the Ottomans. Carrying the parchment close to his heart, the words scrawled across his mind like a dragon declaring his escape. Ferenc wished to don his armor at this very moment, to put a horse between his legs and fly straight at the Ottoman ranks. He arrived in Sárvár while the moon glowed full in the sky. Despite the late hour, as soon as word reached his mother, she rushed to meet him.

"You cannot," his mother said. "You must finish your studies. It is simply not possible."

Ferenc ignored her, passing a detailed list of supplies to a manservant.

"You will be the next Nádasdy baron, you must carry on your father's name. You can't go on thinking you have the freedom to put yourself at risk."

As the manservant hurried off, Ferenc dropped his hands and regarded the woman. Her gray hair, colored the same as her flesh, like the remnants of a crumbling imperial temple. He'd played at being the dutiful son for much too long. He intended to take this opportunity with two hands. "We both know I am not best suited for learning. I don't have the taste for it. But this," he pulled out the parchment from the folds of his overcoat, "this I have the taste for, the yearning for."

He paced, his legs aching for movement, the grip of a blade in his hand.

"Your wedding—"

"Will be here when I return," he finished firmly.

She shook her head. "You can't, your betrothed can't wait."

"We are deeply in love, remember? My betrothed will wait till the end of time if needed," he answered a wry smile curving his lips.

Fire in those old eyes, then respect.

"I will also need a contingent of Nádasdy soldiers to accompany me. Not many, but they must have a thirst to fight the Ottomans. Also horses and one of the carriages," he added.

"We have horses to spare, but we are down one carriage until it is repaired," she answered, swallowing at the air like a fish.

"Repaired?"

She waved her hand. "Some problem with a wheel. It shouldn't take long. The serving man will take longer to repair, I think."

Blinking in confusion, Ferenc almost asked for more, but thought better of it. After all, it really didn't concern him. "We can go without a carriage then."

Her eyes shone with moisture. "I could not bear it if you died." Her voice broke. "Not both you and your father."

Ferenc hid his annoyance. He'd outgrown his need for a mother's tenderness long ago. His entire life he'd waited for this moment and he'd go with his mother's blessing or without. "There are things that must be done, battles to fight and win. I will be the one who wins them."

She exhaled, long, ensuring he would note her despair. "You best go see the Báthory girl before you depart. She will require an explanation on why you cannot wait for a ceremony to bind the two of you before you leave."

He fought the urge to yell. "Alright. I will summon her."

"At a proper hour, I hope," she said.

Ferenc pursed his lips. "Yes, of course."

Let the Ottomans cower before him.

Or whoever spoiled for a fight.

He'd bring them nothing but suffering.

—

Dorottya wandered the woods like a ghost under the moonlight. Lost in the dreams within her head, a portrait of pretty Mirella, decorated and much too pale. A vacant thing, decorated for wearing with no one to do so. She clicked her tongue. Darkness enveloped her where the trees grew thickest, stuffing itself into her mouth like a used rag, forcing her to taste its desolation. "He calls me Dory," she said to the night.

The night did not care.

Where were the blooms?

Odd whines escaped her mouth, rising in shrill chirps, a wounded dog, lost and waiting for hope.

"Ugly," she said.

A tree root stirred, glowing white from what moonlight crept past the canopy. It slithered and she followed.

Come dance.

She heard them, the dancing girls and the old man, all the way out here. His roots caressed her, urging her forward, encouraging. Roots made of marble, running from deep below the castle. Branches slashed her bumpy flesh, thorns found legs and arms to barb and burrow themselves into.

Come dance with us.

Yes, to be worshipped like them. Only the beautiful are

allowed to dance.

"Ugly," she said again, not sure if the wetness on her face were tears or blood.

The old man watched his girls, ripping at their breasts and lifting their skirts like the guard had done to Dorottya. They all snorted like pigs for him.

I will make you pretty.

A clearing came into view, a sweet moonlit place, like magic. In the center a small cabin had grown, ramshackle and filled with mystery.

24

Susanna would leave. The time had come, the Nádasdy's would ensure Erszébet had a companion more befitting of her age. Her charge had taken the girl from the tavern into her service, until of course the baroness found out. Perhaps the older woman would simply shift the girl formally, taking up the room Susanna would have occupied. Erszébet would like that, she loved the music the girl played. A new Elena for Erszébet.

Susanna and Ficzkó would find another path, when he recovered and could travel, they would find a new destiny. She touched the fold in which she had tucked the cross. Perhaps Agoston would help her. The idea made her blush and joyful at the same time. She already wished to see him again.

Susanna climbed the stairwell and a jangle of coins within her gown reminded her of her agreement to Lord Báthory. She had done enough. A wedding would happen soon and the baroness kept Erszébet under such lock and key that there should be little concern. Susanna would tell Erszébet as soon as she reached the apartments.

An overcast gray light peaked through the windows and each step seemed to vibrate the castle. Susanna paused on a landing, trying to slow the quick beat of her heart. The bundled stump of her brother's arm was a sight worse than she wanted to admit and the fever . . . she'd leave once he returned to health, they'd leave.

What if he doesn't? What if he dies? It would be easier.

Guilt overcame her.

The dirt floor of the old stone cottage never really left her, somehow its dampness had ground its way into her skin and soul. A refuge hallowed out by children living on the edge of survival. Ficzkó, four summers her elder, took the mantle of responsibility without a word. They didn't talk much about their father's disappearance, but Susanna imagined the man had found a new life, one made better without the burden of children.

When Susanna turned thirteen, Ficzkó became more than just her brother. He had been both brother and father for so long, it seemed natural he would take on the role of lover. She had been young, so very young.

Then Elek was born.

The old ache returned to her heart. She loved that child more than life itself, more than she loved Ficzkó.

There, the truth. She loved Ficzkó, but how, jumbled around her mind like the remnants of their childhood. Never cruel, but insistent, constant, pressing his desires on her no matter where they went. Their son had been born of that, a beautiful creation.

He'd died of it too.

Ficzkó always said he and Susanna would be together. Life and death in one cocoon.

How could she just leave him? She owed him.

Susanna shook her head. He didn't have that right to her, she never asked for these things he'd done. She wished that she could abandon him here. Run away from him too.

Into the arms of Agoston.

She burned with shame.

Susanna would tell Erszébet after Ficzkó recovered, and then she would take her brother and leave. Finally, free of the service to noble households. Free from taint of highborn affairs.

Susanna's riding boots muffled on the rich carpet of the hall. Erszébet must have heard her as she flew out of her quarters like a hawk to a mouse. The Nádasdy maid, Reka followed suit, along with the girl from the inn, smoothing her homespun attire in discomfort. The sight of them gave Susanna reassurance. Erszébet wouldn't be alone.

"Oh thank God on high," Erszébet rushed to Susanna and threw her arms around her. For a moment, Susanna stiffened with surprise, opening her mouth to speak but hesitated.

"I thought you would have to leave to find a surgeon, or worse." The girl's voice vibrated through Susanna, this girl who was not her daughter. She should have been her daughter. If Erszébet was from her blood, she would be . . . different, not a monster.

"My lady," Susanna said, pulling gently toward some chairs, "I need to speak with you."

A Nádasdy manservant bustled into the wing. The pair turned in equal annoyance at the intrusion.

"Many apologies but I am here on behalf of Lord Nádasdy," the manservant bowed. "My lady, the lord has requested a meeting with you in the courtyard."

Erszébet glared. "Now?"

"Yes, my lady. He waits there for you."

"Last I knew he dwelt in Vienna in the bosom of the Habsburgs. What has brought him home?" The girl huffed as if she'd been a rebuked lover.

The manservant shifted. "I believe that is what he wishes to discuss."

Irritation rolled off of Erszébet, yet Susanna glimpsed the spark of the excited girl within. Finally, the man she'd marry would give her time. See her. Get to know her.

Erszébet put a hand over Susanna's. "You need to rest. I know how much your brother's condition has shaken you."

Susanna raised her eyebrows, opening her mouth to speak, wishing she could let out all the things she had prepared to tell the girl.

But before she could respond, Erszébet turned away, snapping her fingers at her maids, "Accompany me."

———

Under the beech trees of the inner courtyard, Ferenc clasped the fabric of his overcoat. He'd agreed to one condition his mother set, to inform the Báthory girl. A farewell of sorts. But his mind raced, the muscles in his legs ached for action.

The girl surprised him, in the short time he'd been away in Vienna his betrothed had begun her bloom. Magyari had been right, she was beautiful. A shame he had to wait till they married to taste her wares. It wouldn't due to beget a child on her before they were joined. He'd sow elsewhere until then. Every lord had bastards, even his father who had left a few out in town that his mother pretended didn't exist.

The Báthory girl contrasted light and dark. A pale oval face framed by the lush darkness of her hair. When she smiled, her teeth flashed white like porcelain, the ends oddly sharp, he wondered if they nipped when properly aroused. She did not appear sad at the news of his upcoming departure. Instead, a flush migrated to her cheeks from some internal fire.

"Why haven't you arranged to visit me until now? Now that you plan to leave?"

He blinked. "I—

"It is as if you think I am ugly."

Her informality surprised him. "Of course not, my lady."

"And now you go to war."

"I've been called to serve as a commander."

"For the Habsburgs," she sneered.

"It's a matter of perspective." He regarded her critically. "Would you rather I fight for the Ottomans?"

Her dark eyes sucked at his soul. "Don't be ridiculous and don't pretend that this has been foisted on you unwillingly."

Words escaped him.

"You don't want to be here anymore than I do." She locked a gaze on him and moved closer. The heat seemed to have flushed her lips, flushing him.

"The walls close in, they always have." His own admission surprised him.

A predator he realized, hunting her prey. The thought excited him. He glanced at her maids a few steps away, locked in their own conversation, looking to their own concerns. Good.

"Yes," she said, leaning into him her voice low and conspiratorial. "I know, my lord."

Not a girl any longer and so close.

Pushing her body against him, she unfettered his desire, someone who matched him for daring and wishes for freedom. She burned him, heat scorching through their clothing. Without realizing what he did, Ferenc grasped her, tasting the forbidden darkness of the Báthory line, like drowning in dismemberment and ecstasy. He wanted more and he pulled her to him roughly, seeking to bruise her.

She went abruptly unresponsive and stiffened. Ferenc pulled back afraid he had gone too far and the gossips would begin their chirping. It is funny how powerful those little chirps could be.

She made an odd gurgling noise, her eyelids flickering open to the rolling whites of her eyes. Ferenc pushed away and she tumbled unnaturally to the ground twitching, frothy spittle dripped from her open mouth. A maid rushed forward.

Ferenc's stomach soured.

The girl twisted and craned her head and he wanted to push it further, to hear it crack from her spine. Heat left him with a dull ache of disgust at the sickening spectacle of his betrothed, a product of the great house of Báthory. A line of sultry demons, God, this would amount to worse gossips than if he had bedded her right at this spot. She appeared crazed, fluttering about and straining, possessed. He'd be away from here and her soon, but the idea that he must marry her made him nauseous. What a vile thing.

The Báthory nurse, Susanna, appeared, shooing the younger maid, Reka, and gathering up his betrothed like a child. Ferenc's lips twisted in distaste. The nurse was no better, a brittle crone wrapped in a woman's body, as if her insides had aged before her face.

"My lord, it is a sickness. It will pass," the nurse said, her eyes pleading a request for understanding, wafting with the bitter scent of desperation.

Ferenc stood. He hungered.

"Reka, would you please see my lord to . . . wherever it is he needs to go," the nurse said, her face growing haggard and pinched.

The maid tilted her head in acquiescence. Dewy and full bosomed, she led Ferenc from his own inner courtyard, to his own outer courtyard. He almost laughed.

"What again is your name?" He asked.

She blushed prettily against the faint sounds of chaos behind them.

"Reka, my lord," she said.

He leered openly. "Reka," he paused, pretending to taste the name, "I would like very much if you would bring me my meal this evening. I ride to war in the morning and pleasant company would give me strength to fight."

She glanced back and blushed more. "Yes, my lord."

Tomorrow, he would leave to fight the Ottomans and undoubtedly leave both corpses and bastards in his wake.

25

Incessant droplets drenched Dorottya's face. Faux tears, waking her, making her listen again. She sat up, confusion splashing against her mind. Wandering in the dark, she'd fallen into the earth itself. A tunnel ran long and dark from her vantage point. Above, morning light slithered in through an opening.

Driving feet forward, she lurched into the darkness of the tunnel, instinct her only guide in the black. Water dripped like the chime of bells, tinkling and gonging in secret celebration. Step by blind step, she felt her way.

Soon, suffocated daylight shadowed the tunnel ahead and the earthen floor gave way to stone that slopped gently upwards. She ascended, crawling from the soil like an infant intent on its own birth with no regard for its mother. Up and through an arch, she emerged into a shadowy forgotten corner of the courtyard of the castle.

A bubble grew in her belly and she belched up a laugh that rang unnaturally against the bricks. The old man laughed too, rolling thick with phlegm.

See how I will make you pretty?

She trembled with the thought, joy coursing through her veins.

Dance for me, Dory.

Other servants adverted their eyes as she entered the washroom. The hung linens damp with steam. Ficzkó still lay within, his jaw clenched tight in the quiet misery of his fever dreams. His sister had gone but Dorottya could still detect the woman's scent. Sunshine and rot.

She kissed Ficzkó's forehead, letting the sick heat warm her lips.

No one loved him as she did.

When he woke, he'd see.

—

The Nádasdy heir rode away to war and Erszébet rode away in her dreams. Her father, the baroness, they all thought Erszébet didn't know, didn't understand, didn't see. They thought they must cajole and hammer her into place, like a naughty child.

Her quill scratched against parchment. *Dearest Father . . .*

She stopped being a child a long time ago. Acting the part could only be contained for so long. She envied young peasant women, how they could move through the land, see the sunrise with only the day's simple work ahead of them. Nobility engulfed her with responsibility and expectation. Be educated. Be marriageable. Be desirable. Be a breeding mare. Remain unnecessary and replaceable. Be beautiful. Be pure. Noble women were the links to power but remained as helpless as the chickens slaughtered for the evening meal.

She would not be slaughtered.

That ridiculous brother of Susanna's, Ficzkó, had failed in the simple task Erszébet had required. Weaken a wheel of the baroness's carriage, sabotage it just enough so the carriage would falter at high speed, at best the woman would have died trying to follow Erszébet into the countryside. At worst, the carriage would not run. Of course, it had effectively hampered the woman from meddling, but Ficzkó got himself hurt in the process. If the baroness connected Erszébet's involvement . . . she needed to act quickly, something more decisive.

How her head throbbed. Erszébet rubbed a temple in an attempt to clear her vision. The usual would come next, she'd worsen and fall. After that fall, eventually, another time, another place the fall would come again, then exhaustion and more pain before it would clear. Shame made her cheeks burn. A never-ending cycle, until the witch had given her the tincture. She needed that god forsaken tincture. Dropping the quill in frustration, she fought the desire to destroy the room, like she had destroyed Elena.

Splatters of ink ruined the parchment. She'd need to start over, get a fresh sheet. Yet, the splotches gave her pleasure. Ruining something had its own splendor. Like Elena's blood on her dress, across the quaint flowers embroidered by the girl's mother. Dead Elena didn't matter. The girl had been nothing, lowborn and not very pretty, or bright.

Erszébet's head had throbbed in the worst way she'd ever experienced on that day. They locked her and Elena in a room to study. Study, prepare, to know God's word. On the sixth day, God made Adam and Eve. Stupid Eve. Stupid Elena, wouldn't stop badgering about sweet cakes and marriage matches, like a squirrel that chittered and dropped nuts and Erszébet's head hurt so badly. She had to stop the noise.

Blood had mixed with the ink as she made perfect brushstrokes. The best letters she'd ever written, beautiful. Not that her father had seen or cared to look.

Susanna looked. She looked at Elena and she looked at Erszébet's letters and she ran, ran, ran. Stupid Susanna.

Her nurse thought she could leave. Thought that she could just walk away from Erszébet after spending so much time with her, after being the only one who would ever listen or care. But Erszébet knew that no one really cared more about anyone else but themselves. Why would she think that Susanna would be any different?

Erszébet wiped a tear and sniffed. The pain flared flashes of white into her vision. She'd fall very soon.

Leave her alone with these Nádasdy freaks. Maids that would lure her future husband with their pretty little bodies. Bodies that didn't convulse or vomit on their own clothes.

And he just left her there. Walked to war and left her without any other word.

If anyone, anything was going to belong to Erszébet, it would be Sárvár and Ferenc. Every drop of these belonged to her. She'd hold onto them both with all her weapons.

Her mirror agreed, admiring her high smooth forehead, the dark waves wisping around her face like cracks in marble. How powerful beauty could be in the world of men.

Her vision grew dark, the mirror clattered to the floor and she held onto the velvet arms of the chair desperately. Pain seared through her brain, a heat that felt like it would pop her eyes from the sockets. The room faded and a hot air pushed at her hair. Suspended by time, only a hair's breadth of moments before she'd fall.

Apples. The thought made her smile, at least in her aching mind. All of this would be hers.

Her bones jolted into the floor, teeth clamped impossibly tight, spittle leaking down her chin and she jerked across the rug like a possessed thing. Maybe she was a possessed thing. When it eased, her muscles unwinding and turning to putty, she wept.

Done, at least until it happened again. The next one would come soon enough. But in the meantime, there would be apples and she'd wrap those around her in ways never imagined. The idea gave her strength as she faced the headache that always followed.

PART III
POISON APPLES

26

Her ladyship had summoned her.

Not to her apartments, but to a storeroom. Thrilling that her ladyship would call for her little witch, that someone so beautiful wanted someone so horrid near her. The old man rolled his phlegmy cough, his bones creaking as the wind blew this way and that.

He calls me Dory.

Beautiful and pretty and ugly.

Pretty Mirella.

Prettier in the log.

Dorottya laughed. Ilona arched an eyebrow in her direction.

Rotten and stinking Ilona, nothing at all a man would want.

No one had asked about Mirella. No one cared, even that friend of her's, Reka. Pretty Reka. Pretty in a darker way than Mirella. Where Mirella shone like the sun and butter, Reka glowed like the moon. Reka flashed her ankles at Ficzkó, just like Mirella had, even though he wasn't awake to see it. Still asleep and fevered. Soon he'd wake, or not at all.

Dorottya shook herself. She had to meet her ladyship, she'd been summoned.

She passed tapestries and paintings: Warriors pledging their fealty to great lords and ladies; Matthias Corvinus taking Vienna, a crowd gaping at him in awe and wonder; a god of a man.

When Dorottya entered the storeroom, she found her ladyship

sitting on a barrel idly eating an apple alone. Her ladyship burned like a goddess, like Mathias Corvinus. Lady Erszébet Báthory. Beautiful goddess.

The old man agreed. He'd claimed her as his, but her ladyship didn't know it yet.

"How is dear Ficzkó?" The goddess asked.

Dorottya licked her lips, trying to clear the muddle of her thoughts. "He continues to fever." She spent her days trickling water down his throat, hoping he'd take enough to keep alive. At night, Dorottya curled next to him. His feverish heat scalding.

He calls me Dory.

"That is very sad." Erszébet chewed thoughtfully. "I am in need of more tinctures and it seems my runner is, well . . . not awake. I thought I'd ask you for them myself."

Dorottya went cold. "No more," she moaned, beating a fist against her leg.

Erszébet's eyes flickered.

"I'll find more. Just need a little time."

"I am running out of patience."

Dorottya whimpered.

Erszébet took another bite of her apple with soft snap under her teeth. "You are in debt to me. But there is something you can do about it." She held up the fruit and Dorottya obliged, taking a bite from where her ladyship had just fed, like a sweet, succulent union of their lips. Pleasure moved through her, a sonata of worship. "I will tell you how you can repay me, Dorottya Széntes."

Dorottya leaned forward.

"I want you to poison someone." Erszébet pulled another apple from the barrel, its skin glistened black-red. "Using these."

See how I will make you pretty? You can be all of them. All the beauties.

"Who?"

"Do you agree?"

Dorottya shivered. "Oh, yes. I do." Her head bobbed.

"The Baroness Nádasdy. My future mother-in-law. Well . . . if you do well, she would have been my future mother in law."

Dorottya sank her teeth into the apple again, letting the juice seep into her mouth. "I will do this."

"Good."

We can make them all ours.

"Yes." Dorottya's voice came out husky and low.

"In the meantime," her ladyship flashed pearly teeth. "why don't you bring our dear Ficzkó up to one of the empty rooms in my apartments. I think he'll recover much better there, than a washroom."

All of them. All the fairest. Ours.

"Yes, yes, yes."

—

The mud of the encampment fed his imagination. The clang of dancing blades, the siege machines, screams of pain and lengths of innards spilling from the dead and dying, it all left a succulent taste in Ferenc's mouth. Esztergom rose before him, beckoning him to free her from Ottoman hands. The Habsburgs helped furnish troops, most of them Hungarians who served the Habsburg cause, or at least served for the pay. If they died, there would be someone to take their place. Ferenc could see them all on the board, pieces aligned in formations, strings of strategy connecting them, pushing toward the Esztergom fortress.

An Ottoman messenger rattled before him, issuing proclamations and veiled threats.

"You will find, that I am not easily threatened." Ferenc signaled to one of his officers, who nodded and disappeared. "However, had you offered gold, you would find that I am easy to bribe."

His officers laughed. His friend, György Thurzó, clapped Ferenc on the back, the bellow of his amusement rising louder over the scene.

Ferenc grinned. "See how well the Habsburgs have bribed us to kill you?"

"It is sad that you will not see reason." The messenger shook his head. "What would you like me to tell my lord when I return?"

"I do have a message."

"You will lose, you realize," the messenger said, "choose your words wisely and my lord may show you mercy."

György shook his head. "It is a good day for blood."

Ferenc agreed. "Indeed it is."

The officer returned, bearing a package covered in cloth. Ferenc took it, licking his lips as he unwrapped his newest prize. It glinted in the light, a wicked thing, affixed with a series of small blades. He slipped it over his hand. A perfect claw.

"Ottomans know little of mercy. This for example," he held his clawed hand aloft, "I found this in one of your abandoned camps. Left behind, forgotten. A treasure. Now tell me, does this look merciful to you?"

Two of Ferenc's men seized the Ottoman. The man's eyes had gone wide but to his credit he remained calm, clinging to some semblance of civility as if it would save him.

"There is no honor in this," the messenger said.

"What I do will not kill you right away. I will leave you with the capacity to tell your lord my message."

"What will you tell your wife? Your family once you have done this thing? How will you live with yourself?" The Ottoman beseeched, his veneer of calm beginning to crack.

György circled, seriousness pulling at his moustache. "My friend has not yet married. But it is said, his betrothed is crueler than he could ever be."

The mere mention of Erszébet made Ferenc recoil. Even so far from her and home, she still could reach him. A snake playing at being a rose. One day he'd have to be rid of her. One way or another.

"In fact, I think," György said, tilting his head at Ferenc with some amusement, "the girl strikes more fear into my fellow commander here than any man on the battlefield could. But her family is rich and powerful. Suppose it makes it worthwhile."

Ferenc narrowed his eyes. "We are all monsters."

"True. One day, you will need me to deal with your monster," György said. "After, we will drink together and talk of this day, the day which we listened to an Ottoman messenger scream before returning him to his master."

Ferenc clasped György's arm. "I look forward to that day. Now is the time to create that memory we will share."

The messenger flinched. Ferenc brandished the claw and brought his face close to the man, smelling the salt of his sweat. "Here is my message, so you will remember it before the pain comes." Mud squelched under his boots. "Tell your master that the Black Prince of Hungary is coming. And I will hunt you all."

27

A storage room crowded with fine unused things became Ficzkó's sick residence. Furnishings neatly stacked, hewn from dark wood, marble topped or carved with ornate skill, more riches and finery than Dorottya had ever seen in one place and all shut away. Odd how nobles shuttered things of value until minute precise moments, and if they never became useful, they lay forever forgotten under a layer of dust.

Dorottya had seen fit to beat the disuse from the large ornate bed in the corner and piled clean linens and coverlets upon it. She laid Ficzkó down and it seemed to swallow him up, turning the man into something child-like and helpless.

She pulled the covers to his chin and listened to his breath, the steady push and pull of air came relaxed and he stirred slightly. This would be good, allow the full impact of her medicines to work. Perspiration beaded on his forehead, the linens already soaking up the fluid eagerly. He'd need more medicine soon and stronger to push him out of the last of the malaise. He would wake and he'd know that she saved him.

His Dory.

She also needed to poison an apple and the woods beckoned her to return. The old man gifted her with that special passage, the underground byway where she could move to the woods and back to the castle with ease. She'd make good use of it.

She could use many combinations of herbs to infuse in the apple, but the best herb still eluded her. The same flower she desperately sought for Erszébet. She'd need to concentrate the herb further. Lull the baroness quickly into a sleep, unmoving, unable to speak, all the while her body died. Everything Erszébet wanted. Dorottya would grant everything she could to her goddess.

She'd visit Mirella again too. Pretty flowered Mirella.

She wanted to see that she hadn't dreamed the perfection of pale dead flesh.

—

It smelled of rain. Dorottya emerged from the tunnel with a lantern in hand, retracing the path she had taken before, moving through the patches of underbrush and ducking under low branches. She hummed, dreaming up herbal concoctions for killing old noble women. Beautiful apples pricked with the smallest of needles, soaked in a poison-infused bath. That would do nicely.

Up ahead the long log stretched. A patter started, a soft drizzle bouncing from the canopy, falling with tickling fingers. Dorottya stepped carefully over slick moss, feeling for the lip of the massive hollow with her chill fingers. Rain drove faster, the woods echoed the voices of a million leaves and raindrops. A foot slipped, forcing her to focus on balance. Steadied, she brought herself high enough to finally look at the prize within, but the log pulled the shadows into its hollow heart.

She lifted the lantern high, afraid the rain would sputter out the flame. Her eyes tried desperately to adjust with the dimming light. She brought the lantern closer, any closer and she would tumble back down.

She stared.

Her mind grappling with what lay before her.

There was no Mirella, no dead pretty girl.

Dorottya drew a sharp breath.

But the log was not empty. Instead of Mirella, the hollow sprouted with familiar blooms, succulent white even in the yellow of the lantern. Drops of rain making them bow and nod to each other. Their red centers eaten by the dark.

Corpse poppies.
Enough to keep her ladyship happy.
Enough to kill.

———

Erszébet beamed at Susanna, eyes shining bright with excited rebellious plans. "We'll keep him here till he's recovered." She turned to the innkeeper's daughter, who worked at stitching new wrappings for Ficzkó's wound. "Katya will look after him when the witch isn't here. But let's be honest, the witch fancies him, so it's not likely she will be often absent." A laugh escaped Erszébet like a wheeze, her cheeks flushed a zealous pink.

Susanna's insides churned with unease. "My lady," she began, licking her lips, "I'm not sure that is the best, if the baroness were to find him here."

"Then I would be sure to she knew this was your idea," Erszébet said, looking both bilious and coy in her confidence. She paused a moment too long. "Only a jest. No, I'm not so worried over that, but I think"—letting her lashes brush her cheeks in mock modesty—"with your brother so close, you'd never think to leave me at all."

Susanna froze like some silly ice sculpture. She could hear the old woman from town pleading in the back of her mind.

Run.

"Surprised that I know? I'm not a fool. One look of longing when that peasant gave you that little charm." Erszébet sniffed, her voice rising an octave in mockery. "Please, my daughter, please, you never got to be a normal child," she repeated the words Susanna had said in the inn.

Erszébet sauntered closer. "I told you I'm not your daughter, but you are in my service. I am your lady, you will do as I command. You will stay, just as I will stay."

Katya glanced up nervously from a corner.

Erszébet bent closer to Susanna, as if to share some ridiculously shallow secret. "I won't let you leave me," she whispered in her nurse's ear. "No. You cannot leave me. If you think you can, well, you know of exactly what I am capable. We really do want your brother to return to health. These sorts of things can turn for the worst so quickly."

Run.

Erszébet twirled abruptly on the innkeeper's daughter. "What is wrong with your little fingers? Can't you sew one stitch at all?" Erszébet snatched the cloth from the girl's hands.

"Yes, my lady. I mean, no, my lady, there's nothing wrong with my fingers," Katya stammered.

"You're trying to make a mess of these healing linens. You wish you were a noble, don't you? Think you're able to hide those desires from me? Think I can't see how you want what is mine? I can smell it on you, a little dog in heat." The sound of her voice had reached fervor. She spun in the tempo of growing rage.

The hollow pit inside of Susanna opened into a chasm, her limbs barely obeyed. "Please, my lady, won't you come sit—"

"Shut up. I'll decide when I want to sit. You'll know because I'm doing so," Erszébet snapped. "I must be able to deal properly with laziness of those in my employ. God knows who else the Nádasdy's will take from me next. Everyone must be highly skilled and loyal. Are you loyal, girl?" Erszébet glared at the maid.

Katya's eyes widened. "Yes, my lady, of course."

"Let me see your fingers."

The trembling girl thrust her fingers out for inspection as if the quick obedience proved loyalty. Erszébet grasped them tight, squishing three together turning the flesh white.

"I see the problem, yes, clearly. Let me show you. Give me your needle."

Susanna's mind raced, the cliff's edge rapidly approached and she could do nothing but witness the fall.

"Oh yes, right here, here's the problem." Erszébet brought the needle down like a hammer and stabbed the girl's finger. So much noise, Susanna tried to cover her ears.

"Oh no, here's the other one." The girl shrieked and tried to pull away. Another stab, then another. She raised her hands over her head in an attempt to fend off the attacks, but they only became more intense.

"Erszébet!" Susanna shrieked.

The needle found another mark, the eyes the girl tried desperately to cover, her shrill screams mixing with Erszébet's wordless cries of excitement. Blood flecked Katya's face.

"It must have been your eyes. Maybe both the fingers and the eyes." She shoved the needle further into the girl's eye, deep into her head. Nausea collided with Susanna and she grabbed at the wall for support. The needle had disappeared, but Erszébet's fingers had not stopped, they sunk further. The maid made a violent flop and fell silent, twitching under Erszébet's grip. With a long exhale, she finally released the body, pulling her gore covered fingers from the socket.

Susanna tumbled to the floor.

"Really, nurse, you should have more stamina." Erszébet hummed. Susanna recognized the melody in her haze, a song she used to sing to Erszébet when she was small.

Stretch'd her gleaming neck
Like a rush-hidden swan
Like a flower by the beck,
Like a moonlit poplar branch,
Like a vessel at the launch
When its last restraint is gone.

28

Thirst pierced Ficzkó with such a longing he'd never experienced. He opened his mouth, involuntarily searching for a lost teat, fissuring his lips, painfully splitting the dehydrated skin.

"Water," he said so softly that he could barely hear himself. He tasted copper.

From a miserable corner, the soft muffled sound of weeping answered his plea.

Ficzkó cracked open his eyes.

There his sister stood, a slender outline, hair escaping wildly from a braid. She had braced herself against an old ornate bookcase, hand covering her face as if she could catch the fall of each bitter tear.

"Water," he said again with more determination.

Startled, Susanna dropped her arms and gave him an astonished look. A dawning of realization lit her tear-streaked face and she rushed for a pitcher. Within moments she held a saturated cloth to his lips, drippling water over the cracks and into his eager mouth. This was the teat he had been casting about for. It tasted of familiar ash and well water, as delicious as any wine he'd ever drunk.

"I thought you'd never wake up." Susanna wiped her puffy eyes.

"Not dead." He tried to laugh but it came out as a croak.

She glanced at the bookcase, a hard look as if she searched for something. Ficzkó examined his surroundings, an ornate room filled with furniture and other finery, paintings and books. Some covered with linens, others piled against each other and forgotten in their haphazard angles. He lay on a bed in the middle of it all.

A wheeze of a laugh escaped his lungs.

An ache hummed in his shoulder, growing louder and insisting on his attention, he flexed his arm, lifting it to ease the discomfort. A wrongness in the movement caught his attention. Susanna said nothing, gazing down at him with sadness, lines of worry etched across her forehead.

Where an arm should have protruded from the shoulder, there was nothing but a thickly packed nub of flesh. His blood froze.

He had been making cuts to the carriage wheel, weakening it. His eyes widened, and then the carriage rolled backward.

"Dorottya had to remove it." Susanna motioned to where his right arm should have been. "You've been fevered for several days. We weren't sure you'd live." Her lips twisted. "And Erszébet had you brought here to . . . recover."

Erszébet. The name pushed past him like a hot wind. He'd been under that blasted carriage for her. Doing his lady's bidding. What a fool. And the baroness, had she wondered where her little bird had gone?

He paused. "Did the baroness use the carriage?" His voice drew a long gravel to the words.

Susanna seemed to have taken his meaning well enough. Her gaze strayed to the bookcase again before snapping her attention back to him. "No, not after the accident. It is my understanding that she had planned to follow Erszébet to the countryside, not that we knew that beforehand." She gave him an inquisitive look, the tears had dried. "Why do you ask?"

The creak of the door distracted them both and Dory's ugly face led the way into the room. He resented the intrusion, but Dory was such a miserable being that as always, he couldn't help but feel a tang of sympathy. Not for the first time, he wondered what had brought her to this moment in her life.

Dory's drooping and watery eyes moved over him and a smile bloomed on liver lips. Rotting teeth stood out like proud soldiers. She held a plate of food, including several beautiful dark apples. Hunger bubbled within him like a storm.

"Eat slowly," she instructed.

—

Earlier, Susanna had come to Dorottya in a frenzy. On the outside, she moved slow, said little, but her eyes darted and threatened to roll back in her head. She moved in deliberate, desperate attempts to keep her body from bolting.

"We must leave," she said.

"Leave?" Dorottya woke up from her haze.

"I need to get my brother and leave. Please." There were tears in her eyes. "I can't get him out on my own. I need your help. I need—I know we haven't been on the best terms, but I can see how you feel about Ficzkó. I know you'll want him to be safe as much as I do."

His name made Dorottya's heart cramp. A shrill laugh echoed off the courtyard, female, flirtatious, young. Mirella? No, she was dead. Her friend, Reka, maybe. They were so like each other, it was hard to tell them apart. Where did dead Mirella go?

The laugh again. It sounded so much like Mirella, maybe she dreamed the body, maybe it hadn't been there in the first place.

"I don't know who else to turn to. I can't get him safely away without you."

"You think she'll hurt him?" Dorottya tilted her head, resting it against the brick, feeling the cool curvature of the exterior wall like a fish swimming through dead peasant bodies.

"If she has to." She pursed her lips, they were snowy pink. "Eventually she will hurt someone new. It's what she does. He doesn't understand. He won't want to leave."

Dorottya hesitated.

"You only need to get my brother out. Bring him out the gate. They won't question you if you hide him. After that, you can forget about us."

A maid she didn't know strode past an upper level window. Only a flash, an instant, but she could see black hair and milk skin, like a ghost or a vision. Dorottya moved her tongue, trying to moisten her mouth. "What if I want to go with you? With Ficzkó?"

What if Dorottya could pull on that skin? What if she could button herself inside of perfection. What difference was that to a fancy gown?

"Then we'd travel together if you wish." Susanna held a hand to her stomach, as if to settle a war within her guts. The woman never looked very well, but now it seemed a wind could blow her away.

"Yes, yes. I'll help."

Susanna stood straight and breathed loud, letting out tendrils of shadow with the exhale. Dorottya could almost see the air that had been inside her twisting, twisting with fear before giving over to the atmosphere of Sárvár.

"I know a secret way out. In two nights," Dorottya continued. "I will put him to sleep and smuggle him out in a cart. You'll need to bear him into the woods. It will take some time for the sleep to wear off."

Susanna nodded, hope returning some color to her lips and cheeks. She must have been beautiful once, in the days of new womanhood. Now, she looked taut and forgotten. Like a dried rose, ready to crumble at the merest touch.

"Be there when the moon is high."

"Yes." She looked at Dorottya directly for the first time and tried a soft smile, but her eyes still shimmered with unshed tears and shielded revulsion. "Thank you," she mouthed.

She turned and stopped after two steps, twisting back. "Will you be leaving with us then?"

She didn't want Dorottya to come, only wanted the usefulness. Dorottya could hear it in the unsteady gravel of her voice. A taint of old wariness.

"I haven't decided yet."

She cast her gaze downward in shame, as if she sensed Dorottya knew her thoughts.

They don't want you. No one wants you.

Ugly.

Words seeped into the soft places of her soul and killed spirit-tissue as they went.

"In two nights."

"When the moon is high," Susanna confirmed, before passing through the colonnade and into the apartments of the nobility.

—

Susanna snuck out of the castle and crossed into Sárvár town, her feet seemed to know the way, as if those appendages were smarter than her head. Maybe they were. She couldn't leave without telling Agoston. The cross jingled against the coins in her dress.

For Ficzkó to be entombed in that room of all rooms—where had the book gone? He couldn't have taken it from the shelf. A maid? The witch?

An edge of panic rose with her thoughts, a wild beast of fear.

She forced herself to breathe slowly. Ficzkó had woken. He'd be alright. She'd get him out of there and they would escape.

She had sent word to Agoston and relief flushed through her veins to find him already in place, waiting, his grim expression made more serious by a sheen of a patchy beard. As she approached, his eyes told another story, twinkling with mischief and desire. Her heart jumped into her throat and seemed to flutter there like a trapped butterfly.

"My lady," he bowed.

"Stop that," Susanna said instinctively, feeling the creep of heat flush over her cheeks, she looked away.

"Pardon my confusion." A corner of his mouth turned up with wry humor.

She had tried to dress plainly, thinking she would blend in, but the cloth was too finely woven, the skirts unmuddied. A long way from the stone cottage where she and Ficzkó had grown up. What had she become since?

"I am leaving my ladyship's service," Susanna blurted.

Agoston straightened.

"Something's happened," she drew a breath, "I'm afraid and I don't know anyone enough to ask for help. I know that you barely know me."

"It's alright, hey, you're shaking," Agoston pulled her alongside him. "What is it? What's happened?"

Susanna shook her head. "I just know that I need to get away and I need to get my . . . brother away."

"Brother?" Agoston raked a hand through his hair. "Where will you go?"

Susanna slumped. "I don't know yet."

Agoston gripped her shoulders, pulling her closer and forcing her to lift her chin. "You'll think I'm crazy, but come with me.

Just come to the shop."

"I don't know why, but I want that more than you can imagine," she said, gazing up at his concerned face.

Realization dawned over his features and despite the increasing darkness of sunset around them, his eyes seemed made of light.

"But first," Susanna started before he said more, "I need to make sure both my brother and I are away. I don't think we can stay in Sárvár, she'd find us much too easily then."

"She? Ah, it doesn't matter, the woods perhaps? There's an old cabin. I can take you there."

A pang of hope filled her. She wanted to leave Ficzkó and flee right this moment with Agoston. Erszébet wouldn't even know until the morning or when she suddenly craved mother-like attentions. Then again, she could be looking right now. Susanna went cold at the thought.

Erszébet would kill Ficzkó, just to punish Susanna, and mount his head somewhere she'd see it day in and day out. "Yes," Susanna said, "that would work."

"When?"

"Meet here in two nights' time?"

He pulled her into him and she went willingly, bending like a blossom in the spring breeze. He kissed her with an earnest simplicity that made her feel safe. She'd never felt safe before. When Ficzkó kissed her, it always tasted of possession.

This . . . she leaned into him, breathing in his scent, this was so different, this tasted of happiness.

29

Red apples like fresh blood, then black ones like scabs. How difficult for Dorottya to resist picking at their skins, tearing them open to gaze at the pale flesh beneath. Choosing the darkest one, she held it up in the firelight. Such a fine thing. The needle pierced flesh with delicate precision. Tiny canals for the poison to enter.

She dropped the apple carefully into the bowl and a petal rocked in protest on the infusion's surface. Many blooms had gifted their red centers making the infusion just potent enough to kill and to kill quickly.

More work ahead, tinctures to brew and poultices to pack, the busyness gave her a sense of purpose. And a girl, Katya, to bury. On the pallet, the body of her ladyship's newest maid rested, a coin replaced the missing eye. Dorottya bent over the body, peeling back the flap of flesh to reveal the girl's cavernous torso packed with herbs. A homely and poorly fashioned doll nestled in the girl's neck. Hem lines, from the soldier's linen shirt she'd used to sew the thing, striped its face crookedly as if it bore scars from war. Dorottya lifted the doll and pushed it unceremoniously deep into the bed of herbs and flesh.

The girl didn't speak to Dorottya, didn't whisper things like the old man did. But she'd have a purpose.

The old man crouched in the corner, blue skin almost gray, so

filled with promises. He nodded.
Your mother called me, just like you do.
She wanted beauty too.
So I gave her you.

30

Ficzkó twisted against the pillows and let out a drowsy sigh. With the fever gone, Dory arranged a bath, fresh clothes and linens. She left him, finally, her gray face eclipsing the sunlight in some other part of the castle. Honestly, all the attention put him in a pleasant mood, even if it came from Dory, but particularly the tears Susanna shed for him—that she hadn't thrown him away, not like their father had.

Their father hadn't left to find work. After watching their mother and neighbors waste away from sickness, he fled like a scared animal. Ficzkó didn't run. Never. He'd always take care of Susanna. But he had to admit, this chamber, a real bed, it certainly didn't hurt to enjoy the perks of illness while he could. Let Susanna fret, just a little.

He stretched his arms and gazed at the ornate woodwork on the ceiling, before realizing only one arm was truly there, the other a figment of his memory. The packed nub ached at the reminder and so did the swirl of emotions in his heart. He dozed in and out of wakefulness until the room turned to blackness of night. A shuffle brought him from his healing dreams, the sound of someone shifting their weight across the room. Ficzkó's breath caught. Rats, he thought. They invaded everywhere, even the rooms of the powerful.

His scalp prickled and hair raised. The shuffle changed into a jog and Ficzkó opened his mouth to scream.

Nothing rose from his lips. The thing stopped at the side of the bed. Ficzkó sensed it looming over him, maliciousness saturated the air.

Suddenly, the door creaked open. Light illumined the painful darkness, chased the evil. Only empty air surrounded his bedside. Erszébet stole into the room with a candle in her hand and a wicked smile on her face. Ficzkó could have kissed her in relief and it seemed that she had something similar in mind. Her eyes glittered.

"We must talk," she said.

He cleared his throat, trying to muddle through the cotton of his mind.

She put down the candle on a table and stepped forward.

"Your sister is plotting to leave," Erszébet said simply.

He snapped up, leaning on his one good arm. "What do you mean, leave?"

Lulling her head to one side, she gazed down at him. "She met a man in town. I can see it all over her. She'll run away with him, sooner or later."

"What? Who?" Ficzkó's mind swirled, hot and cold with anger and dread.

"Some peasant. That doesn't matter." She sat on the bed. "What matters is that she doesn't leave and she won't, as long as you stay."

"She wouldn't leave me," he said in disbelief, "we've always been together."

"Of course not," Erszébet soothed. "And after your failure with the baroness's carriage, I want to be sure that you make it up to me."

Her voice was dark and rich and he felt himself responding to her closeness. The memory of the last time he'd been in a chamber alone with her, the whispers of promises he made to do the girl's bidding and his desire kindled into flame. Jealousy hummed in the background of his senses and only served to fuel him more. "What do you want me to do?"

Every inch of the girl had grown into wild lushness like a creature being hunted. A primal and thrilling prize.

"All you have to do is to stay here."

She drew off her cloak, letting it fall to the floor, her body flickered pale in the candlelight. The moon ghosted with icy light.

His breath caught.

"Will you do this?" She crawled toward him. "You owe me."

"Yes." His voice escaped in a hiss.

She glowed, as if her pleasure had already crested and left her in high flush. "Never leave."

"I won't. I'll stay, especially for this," he said as she slithered over him. His ghost hand reached for her and he cracked a grin. "You know, it'll take me forever to recover with all this activity."

She laughed.

He did too.

Her glorious hair ran down her pale flesh like liquid night. A familiar thrill of conquest went through him. He should have lost an arm years ago.

He traced a circle on her back.

"How well do you know your sister, really?" Erszébet grinned impishly at him.

"What kind of question is that?"

"The kind a lady asks her servant."

"Apologies, my lady." Ficzkó pulled her to him and with some clumsiness rolled her beneath him. "Do you do this with all your servants?"

Erszébet squirmed. "Only the faithful ones. Are you faithful, Ficzkó?"

"The most faithful, my lady."

"Then tell me what you will say if she begs you to leave with tears in her eyes."

"I will say," Ficzkó moved urgently against her, "I cannot and do not . . . want to go . . . anywhere away from this."

"Good, servant," Erszébet purred.

—

Dorottya stepped through the east gate under a crescent moon that dangled like a pendant on the neck of the night herself. She'd finished her task, she'd done as her ladyship wanted. She'd always do as her ladyship wanted. Muscles corded in her back as a reminder of the labor, fatigue settling in her bones, and she glowed.

"There's the witch."

That voice made Dorottya quiver. She'd thought he'd gone to war with the Nádasdy Lordling. Her soul twisted, trying to escape her body, to run away faster than her flesh could carry her. But she knew that voice better than her own.

"Don't you stay down, pig woman?"

The strike came from the shadows faster than she could have ever hoped to react. The ground hugged her coldly and the moon promised revenge.

The dancing girls took up a tune and shuffled their feet over the cobbles in a jerky dance. Faces decorated with jewels and lace, pretty branches of mistletoe protruding from their skulls, tangling in free flowing hair.

Dorottya rolled, gasping. The soldier's face loomed. His name was Janos.

He pulled back, sucking at his own spittle.

A grin split her face. "Are you missing a shirt?"

Ugly.

The dancing girls sped with the music, heads lolling.

Phlegm landed on her cheek and she laughed.

"Crazy witch."

He left her, wallowing and laughing in the dirt. She didn't know how long she stayed, watching the dancing girls, long after their heads rolled from their shoulders.

He calls me Dory.

She crawled back to her quarters with a sense of victory.

31

Sounds of bustle and horses drew Susanna to the window overlooking the courtyard. Below, the Nádasdy servants descended on a congregation of riders bearing the Báthory standard. The baroness stood below, so rarely seen outside her quarters or meeting hall, and called orders. A horse snorted in response, even the Báthory steeds bucked at the woman's need for control. In the center of the throng, a man called to the baroness.

No ordinary delegation.

The baroness curtsied. "Welcome to Sárvár, my Lord Báthory."

The man dropped his cowl.

Susanna's eyes widened. Erszébet's older brother, Stephen, handed his reins to a servant before dismounting. He strode easily, with the same air she identified with Erszébet. Without needing to see more, Susanna rushed to her charge's room. The girl bent over a desk, scratching with a quill, brow knitted in aggravation.

"My lady," Susanna said, breathlessly.

"What is it?" Erszébet didn't look up.

"There's a delegation from Écsed." She gulped. "Your brother is with them."

Erszébet snapped her attention fully on Susanna, a stormy fury in the dark eyes. "And the baroness?"

"In the courtyard, greeting him."

The girl's mouth twisted. Susanna's body became rigid like a bowstring pulled taut and she pushed away memories, recent and old, with a sick feeling. Tomorrow night, she reminded herself. She'd be away from this cursed place and this cursed child.

The Nádasdy maid, Reka, entered meekly and Erszébet's gaze lingered on the girl a moment too long.

"We'll act as if we were not aware of his arrival," Erszébet said. "Reka, you are to take a message to the witch. Tell her it is time to ready my gift."

Possibilities swirled around in Susanna's mind, but what the girl meant by the message had little meaning to her and she dared not ask.

Erszébet returned to her writing.

"Yes, my lady," Reka said with a stiff curtsy.

———

They waited in silence for what seemed like hours. Susanna wondered if the Nádasdy maid had delivered the message and what it meant. Even more, she wondered if Reka speculated about the innkeeper's daughter. For all Susanna knew, Reka had been the one to get rid of the tortured body.

Erszébet pointedly ignored her nurse and Susanna watched as the girl produced a new tincture bottle. The sight no longer alarmed, instead a sort of relief rushed to take its place. Maybe the tincture would save Reka. Or her. Or her brother for that matter.

Heavy thuds shook the door and Susanna jumped more jarringly than even she expected, as if she had been coiled tighter and tighter while they waited. Susanna opened the door to a manservant, his face flushed with exertion, his big boots offending the colorful birds of the chamber rug.

"My lady," he said with a quick bow, his breath came fast, "your brother is arrived."

Erszébet didn't put down the quill. "This man says my brother is arrived. Susanna, isn't that the funniest thing because it simply is not possible as my brother is in Écsed?"

"Very amusing, my lady," Susanna dutifully agreed.

"Although, I suppose you wouldn't come huffing here with a lie." Erszébet paused in midstroke. "When?"

"Midmorning."

"And here it is late into the afternoon. Why was I not informed?" Erszébet stood, passing the parchment to Susanna, who laid it out carefully to dry. The words drawn large, looping on themselves, like snakes trying to choke one another.

"I was only just sent now to inform you," the manservant bumbled.

Erszébet's face masked the fire Susanna knew it contained, her eyes, so well regarded for their large liquid darkness were now the pits of Hell itself.

"Lady Nádasdy plans a fine meal and asks for your attendance," the manservant continued.

"Please inform my brother that I was not notified of his imminent visit, so my arrival to dinner will be prolonged."

The manservant bowed. "Yes, my lady. Shall I inform the baroness as well?"

An odd smile snapped over Erszébet's face. "Do that. Tell her that I am so happy to finally share a meal with the benefactor of my new home."

Her glittering eyes followed the man as he took his leave. "Fine time for my father to send Stephen to me now. Sold me off and tried to forget me. I think they will find that I won't melt away so easily."

———

Erszébet's gleaming hair pooled black around the cap in an elaborate array of twists, her brows raised confidently over red lips. She donned a gown of simple scarlet, a brocaded bodice with a plunging neckline. Her fingers sparkled with not only the Báthory house ring, but an impressive array of rings fitted with red stones. Susanna followed her charge down the hallway. Her own gown, less fine, fit her position suitably, with its subdued shades of brown.

As Erszébet entered the private dining hall, Stephen rose to his feet. He glittered in the way only Báthory's could, his dark hair, well-oiled, ended in an equally well-groomed beard. Young-faced and broad shouldered, he smirked at his sister as if he knew all her secrets. Perhaps he did.

"There is my dear future daughter-in-law. Such a lovely sight," Lady Nádasdy said, her lined face feigning affection.

"I hope I haven't kept you all waiting for long," Erszébet said, finally taking her seat.

Stephen remained standing, leering at her. "You are not as you left us, sister," the man said, fingering his beard. "Taller."

Erszébet's eyes flashed the same scarlet as her dress. "Yes, it has been some months. Enough time to grow up."

"Lady Erszébet is quite the student, I've been told," Lady Nádasdy said, glancing at Magyari who nodded in happy agreement.

Erszébet did not respond, nor did she take her eyes from Stephen who matched her glare for glare. The table groaned with tension as they waited for the girl to decide which direction to take the mood. Not even Susanna could guess what Erszébet would choose.

Stephen took his seat with a shrug.

Servants brought platters of food and poured a plethora of golden Tokaji wine. A delicate plate of carp, smothered in a sauce of paprika, was placed before her.

Suddenly, Erszébet flashed a wan smile, leaning toward the table, ignoring the food. "How is father? What is the news from Écsed?"

Putting down his cup, Stephen darkened. "Father is dead."

Susanna's stomach dropped.

Erszébet sat as if she had been turned to stone. "Was it a skirmish?"

Her brother barked a laugh. "Would it be so, dear sister. No, he died shivering in his bed. At least that is what his mistress reports." Stephen pierced the flesh of the carp, eagerly spooning it to his mouth with a hearty appetite.

Lady Nádasdy ate with more reserve, her movements as tight as her demeanor. She smiled pleasantly enough, but Susanna thought she could see the dislike in her eyes. This woman played the courteous host well in the presence of Stephen, now the new lord of the powerful Báthory estate.

"You understand what that means, my dear," Lady Nádasdy said.

No one mourned the man, least of all his daughter. Despite

this, clearly Erszébet had not been prepared for the news. The father that barely paid her any mind had died. Susanna knew that his presence gone from this world meant little to her charge, but his death did portend other matters. It meant changes. Big ones. One in particular.

"I'm eager to move forward with the Nádasdy-Báthory union," Stephen said, his mouth full. "There is word of a new push by the Sultan and I'd much rather have all matters settled before we give into a larger conflict."

Lady Nádasdy shook her head. "If it's not the Sultan, it's the Emperor. When will Hungary ever belong to itself again?"

"We must be vigilant and smart." Stephen paused, thoughts turning inward. "We will fight till the last man. I hear good news of the young Lord Nádasdy's success on the battlefield. It seems we have chosen an excellent husband for my sister."

Throwing out a genuine smile, the baroness perked up, her chest visibly swelling. "Thank you, my lord."

"I will be married soon, then." Erszébet interrupted, her voice monotone.

Stephen chuckled. "Yes, sister. Quite. Within the month if we can manage it."

"We must increase your lessons. We will see that you are as ready as possible to run the Nádasdy estates." Lady Nádasdy held her cup in Erszébet's direction.

The girl spooned a delicate morsel to her mouth, her back rigid, face haughty. "Planning to hand me the castle the moment we are wed? Really, Lady Nádasdy, I had no idea you were retiring so quickly."

"Erszébet," Susanna hissed before she could stop herself.

Lady Nádasdy held up a hand. "Lady Báthory," she sucked in a breath and put a finger to her temple, "you are young. I understand that it is a difficult thing to be young and to see just how important these things are. I am trying to prepare you as best as I can. It won't be long before the Ottomans are at our lands again."

Erszébet sipped her wine. "That is why I will have Ferenc, of course. He can teach me whatever it is I need to know. Don't you trust him to ensure his wife is taught properly?"

Stephen smacked the table with a mocking laugh. "Who do you think will be off fighting the Sultan? What kind of time do you think he'll have for lessons of household management? The only lessons he should be working on are those used to beget heirs and combat."

Erszébet glared at her brother. "Almost every moment I have been in Sárvár has been in the shape of lessons. I speak and read Greek, Latin and German as if I was born to these languages. I know how many chickens Sárvár needs for one month, the best crops produced in the fields east of here and how much the people want to love their lords and ladies. Isn't that enough?"

Lady Nádasdy's mouth set in a straight line, the pink of her lips barely visible. She looked tired, worn out with some burden no one could see. "No child, it won't be enough. It'll never be enough."

Susanna engrossed herself in moving around the sauce-soaked capers on her platter. The dealings of lords and ladies didn't include her, a world much bigger than herself. Wait patiently in the background until she could get Ficzkó and leave. The thought made her almost ashamed, but the truth of it saturated her. She wanted to run from the girl she raised as her own. Run as far and away as she could.

"And what would father have said about a hurried wedding?" Erszébet asked, her expression suddenly wounded, her voice soft.

"He'd say hurry, we need unity. The crescent moon and the double-eagle will peck us to pieces soon."

Perhaps, Susanna thought, Erszébet wasn't the only one who had grown a bit—one blossoming into murderous womanhood, the other emerging into cold leadership. Perhaps these roles were more thrust upon them instead of grown into.

Servants cleared plates in preparation for the next course.

"They've done that long before now," Erszébet shot back. "What is our kingdom but carrion picked at by the two over and over again?"

Magyari cleared his throat. "The Lady Báthory has expressed an affinity for the Hungarian cause."

"Has she?" The baroness asked, her tone nondescript.

Magyari gulped golden wine and hastened to add, "which we only study once she excels at all else concerning household management."

"For the interest of my future husband, of course." Erszébet inclined her head. "He also expresses a certain affinity."

Stephen laughed. "Well said, sister."

Tension knotted the air and Susanna could not be sure if her own anxieties had created it, or the play at dinner conversation. Erszébet did not touch her wine and had only barely eaten from the plates brought before her.

Remembering Agoston's soft eyes brought Susanna some peace, a promise of a new start. His sweet and tender kiss. She tried to focus on the idea to keep herself from crying.

New plates, filled with cakes swimming in honeyed cream, paraded into the dining hall. Reka followed suit, holding her own plate of something quite different. At its sight, surprise and foreboding filled Susanna. A chord of wrongness plucked at her heart. Upon a fine porcelain platter, the maidservant balanced a single apple, a gorgeous fruit. And Susanna knew its source immediately.

The maidservant diverged from the servants, bringing the platter like an altar offering, setting it before the baroness. The older woman puzzled at the perfectly formed fruit before her. Its sheer simplicity made the dessert cakes appear overdressed.

Erszébet raised a glass to the baroness. "Please accept my humble gift. The finest fruit from the finest orchard of Sárvár."

Stephen settled back into his seat, wordless in his observations, unreadable eyes glittering like gemstones.

Magyari murmured absent approval.

"I . . ." The older woman's eyes flashed with dull appreciation but also something else . . . distrust.

Susanna remembered the orchard well, and the farmer who Erszébet had bought the apples from. They were indeed delicious, the best she'd ever tasted, as well as the most beautiful and this one was no exception. Perfectly spherical, it shone a glossy midnight that warmed in the candlelight with deep undertones of scarlet. Her heart fluttered and she looked toward her charge. Erszébet's lips parted, her eyes darkly luminous.

"From Sárvár you say?" The baroness said.

"Yes, we chanced upon the orchard while I visited the countryside. The farmer had perfected the fruit you see here, midnight lady he called it. Sweetest flesh I've ever tasted. I hoped you would also find it enjoyable."

"Shall I slice it for you?" Reka asked.

The baroness glanced up, hesitation melting, she let out a soft laugh, a tinkling like faraway bells, as distant as the woman's girlhood. "No, I think not. I will enjoy the fruit like a country woman." She gripped the apple, feeling the shape and weight of it. "Remarkable," she muttered. Her teeth sunk deep into the skin with a satisfying snap, and the woman chewed, her eyes bright.

Susanna's heart sunk. A sense of horror moved through her. Erszébet beamed, bared her teeth in ghastly faux appreciation.

The baroness swallowed and for a breathless moment, Susanna fooled herself into believing that she misread Erszébet.

"At first I thought perhaps you had overstated the gift, but truly, my dear, this is the best apple I have ever tasted. Midnight lady, you said?" The baroness eagerly sunk her teeth into the fruit again.

"Oh yes," Erszébet responded.

"Dare I hope that your time at Sárvár has finally taught you courtesy." The baroness cradled the apple. "See, Lord Báthory, this has been good for your sister."

Stephen's eyes flickered toward Erszébet. "Somehow I doubt that."

Dragons knew dragons.

"Let us set a date for the event," the baroness chittered on. "Perhaps just before Christmastime. Any military campaigns should be on hold then. I have always loved the beauty of winter."

"Excellent choice, my lady," Magyari said, gesturing at Erszébet, "white as snow and filled with purity to match."

The table quieted. How much did the baroness know? Stephen did of course. The statement must have rung as painfully ironic to him as it did to Susanna.

Red as blood.

A heart black as a raven.

Beautiful and horrible.

Susanna shivered and stared at her untouched plate.

"It sounds as good a time as any," Stephen said.

The baroness put a hand to her head. "Good, it is settled then. I will send wo . . ." The woman trailed off, her complexion draining of blood.

"Are you alright, my lady?" Erszébet asked, sweetly.

The apple dropped and rolled across the floor as the baroness wilted. "I am not feeling well." She beckoned for a servant.

Reka moved to the woman's side, her face filled with concern.

"My lady?" Magyari said, peering over his wine.

"Please excuse my hasty withdrawal, I believe I must retire. Age has its limits," the baroness tried to smile, but her lips only wobbled.

Servants fussed over the older woman, helping her rise, intent on guiding her from the room.

"Yes, my lady," Stephen said, rising in courtesy as they half-carried the woman away.

The candlelight danced spots in Susanna's vision. She didn't dare look at Erszébet now, but she already knew the look of victory the girl held.

"Excuse me," the reverend said, rising to follow.

A clatter sounded down the hall and a shout of urgency.

"Sounds dreadful," Erszébet murmured.

Stephen sat down, looking rather comfortable and sleepy. "Pity for those who get in your way. Ferenc will certainly return quickly."

"House Nádasdy will need us all the more," Erszébet said.

"Us?" Stephen mused.

"Brother, do not toy with me. I am, and always will be a Báthory, no matter where and to who you ship me off to."

"He's been named a count, for his war efforts," Stephen said.

With a quizzical expression, Erszébet sipped her wine.

"Your betrothed, I mean. They call him the Black Captain."

Footsteps ran down the hall, jarring, each strike of boots on the stone floor made Susanna tremble.

More shouts. "Get a healer. Fetch the witch, she can help."

Her stomach flip-flopped, forcing her to gag and cough.

Erszébet's face bloomed like a flower exuding perfume. "Is that so?"

Stephen nodded. "You want something."

"For myself and my soon to be husband, this Black Captain. I want the Báthory name. Let Nádasdy fade away with the mother in the hall. Insist that he take the Báthory name, while I keep it."

Someone wept in the hall. Magyari's voice rose in prayer.

Stephen stared hard at his sister. "Not an easy thing to arrange."

"What other choice will my dear Ferenc have?"

He rubbed his chin. "Not much at all. He will need heirs as quickly as he may get them."

"Indeed."

"Why, sister? What drove you to all this?"

Erszébet stood up, putting her hands on the table, she leaned toward him. "No one will forget me again. I want my name to be first on the lips of memory before any man of Hungary."

Stephen let out an appreciative chuckle. "I doubt that."

Susanna focused only on gulping air, in and then out again. She couldn't have imagined Erszébet being able to arrange this, to have so deftly and swiftly changed the rules of power. How did Susanna not see this? How had she been so blind over and over again? She needed Agoston, to run into his arms like she used to run to Ficzkó and lay her head on her new pillar of strength.

Magyari crashed into the room, breathless and red-faced. "The baroness is dead."

The amusement faded from the Stephen. Slowly he raised his glass to his sister. "To the fairest." His voice hissed like steel. "To Countess Erszébet Báthory."

32

The witch had watched Reka. This perfect maid, lithe and shapely, ankles flashing in the moonlight, come here to collect a gift for the baroness. The witch handed her the cloth-wrapped apple. And then the girl ran off again into the inner rooms of the castle, like a child being eaten by a bear.

How that pretty little soul would be filled with sin after tonight, being the hand that brings such gifts. And then, one day, the same maid will swim with the tree roots too, like everyone else.

Returning to her tiny workshop, the witch swung the cracked door closed. While it did little to keep the cold out, it provided a screen from curious eyes. The innkeeper's daughter waited. So patient and kind, the girl sat in the one rickety chair, staring into the tiny empty hearth. The witch didn't feel the cold as much anyhow and she knew how much Katya preferred it. Long tresses were in need of brushing and plaiting, so the witch got to work, humming the same melody to which the dancing girls ceaselessly bounced and giggled. They could drive her insane at times, when the old man did not rein them in. Girls needed a firm hand.

"Shoo," the witch said, pulling much too hard on the maid's hair. It came out in a clump in clenched fist.

Forcing her fingers to relax, she stared as the strands fell away one by one, floating gently to the dirt floor. She must do better, be gentle. It wouldn't do to hurt the girl. She ran the brush down the length of the waves, working through elaborate braids.

The witch fed the girl bits of apple until the mouth did not close on its own, so she worked her needle through flesh and nails through bone. She finished her work with a stain of berry juice on Katya's lips.

Ready for their journey.

A gust of chill wind whistled under the door and the witch pulled the innkeeper's daughter out into the night. She dragged the girl on and on through copses of trees that stood sentry along the town's edge, passing the empty darkened road and into the tall reed grasses. The girl whispered here, like a dream of harlots telling secrets of their nights with kings. Pulling her to the riverside, where the water babbled louder, the witch readied to part with Katya. After all, curses needed sacrifice.

Not the prettiest. Not at all perfect. But she'd do for now.

In the darkness, the stars peered at the pair and winked knowingly. The witch closed her eyes against the immensity and pushed. Into the water with a soft splash the innkeeper's daughter fell.

Now fed, the river quieted. The baroness would soon do much the same. Janos too.

And mother.

The witch turned back for home.

Shouts and alarm among the awakened serving staff. The witch smiled and nodded to herself. She pulled at the door of her tiny room, shutting it again, almost forgetting that Katya no longer lived here.

No longer did that maid sit in the chair, only strands of her hair scattered into the dirt. As the witch turned she found another companion upon the chair. A book, opened to the blue devil, his tongue flicked out from the pages, caressing her cheek. *Make you pretty too.*

The dancing girls stopped, crowding around the witch and the old man, crushing them, tighter and tighter, they spun together. Ribbons streamed and the witch surged with hope and joy. They leaned into her, draping across her body like beautiful fabrics. Their faces stretched against her chest, a bodice embroidered with screams and melodies, their legs rustled into the length of a skirt so full that a thousand folds formed like secret nooks.

—

Susanna dared not pack in any obvious fashion, so not to raise Erszébet's suspicion. But she had sewn pockets into her gown and into these she shoved a few crusts of dry bread. She would have added apples, but she could not bring herself to pick up the fruit. She had no concept of how far into the woods they would travel, but surely Agoston could hunt for them.

Erszébet's brother had left with his delegation that morning, returning to Écsed and pressing Báthory matters. There would be an announcement for the wedding soon and the Báthory house would arrange it. A rider had already been dispatched to give summons to Ferenc. None of the servants spoke, keeping the same hushed tones and efficiency that allowed them to survive under the baroness. What Erszébet would do next, no one could be certain. She had no technical claim to the household without marriage. But it appeared that would happen in short order.

Susanna's charge rarely spoke to her now, and had kept Reka outside Ficzkó's quarters during the day. It became clear that Erszébet also spent her nights within, a perfect excuse to ensure her prey did not escape. Little chance Susanna had to even speak with him and tell him of the ongoings of the castle. A stab of jealousy cut through her stomach. How could he? How could Ficzkó consent to anything with Erszébet? How could he not see the child she had been?

But she knew the answers. Susanna trembled and wished to flee, instead of thinking of the toddler who once ran to her with shouts of joy. From the moment the first needle pierced that poor maid's flesh, Susanna struggled to summon the warm memories of Erszébet's childhood.

Tonight, they'd make their escape. The witch would come through. After all, she loved Ficzkó. And if the witch escaped with them too, so be it. A chill ran along Susanna's spine at the thought.

She tried to contain all her nervous energy. Be ready to move when the time had come at last. A long while yet and who knew what this day would bring. Unsure what else to do, she sat in her small room. The sun rose, a mere ember in the chill sky. Susanna held Agoston's cross tightly and tried to dream of happiness.

Please. Please wait for me.

33

The castle routine moved through the day in an eerie calm. A few of the older servants muttered and shook their heads, but no doubt they'd been there for much of their lives, having seen a great deal already. Somewhere within, the baroness's body had been washed and Reverend Magyari prayed over it, so his god would look kindly on the noblewoman.

Evening fell early, the days shortening, bringing with it the kind of cold that pierces the flesh and worms into the marrow. The witch rose with the darkness. The agreed upon time had come. She'd help Susanna, not because of the woman but because Ficzkó . . . she sighed. Thinking of him somehow made the old man fade, her thoughts clarify and, of course, her heart warmed with excitement.

She chose the prettiest two apples. Ficzkó wouldn't notice the pinholes that pierced its flesh. Unlike the baroness's fruit, this one held much less potency, but enough to make him sleep for the night. The heavy velvet of the shadows made the witch intoxicated and a thrill went over her, that Ficzkó would consume something she had so carefully crafted, as if he would be consuming her too.

Everything moved quieter in the dark as if the veil muffled the sharpness of living. No doubt, Susanna already waited for the witch to bring Ficzkó. The man had mostly recovered, but certainly had been enjoying his time abed. She warmed. He'd have to know by now, know who really loved him. She saved him before and now she'd do the same for him again. Tonight, she'd present herself. She'd be beautiful, just to him. He'd see beyond and love her too.

Padding into the hall, the witch caressed the door. Her love lay just on the other side. She breathed longingly, letting the smile overtake her lips, she pushed open the door. Ficzkó sat up from his bed, his eyes languid, and then paused before throwing an uncertain smile. "Dory, I wasn't expecting you." *He calls me Dory.*

Breathless and eager, her cheeks burned in pleasant warmth.

He shifted beneath the covers. "You really should be asleep at this hour."

"Shhh," the witch said, pulling out the apple, offering it as if her hand was an ornate platter and the fruit the flesh of some roasted beast.

His face twisted. "That is kind, but, well the truth is that I haven't even had a chance to eat the one you brought days ago." He nodded in the direction of the fruit on the windowsill. It looked forlorn, forgotten and dry.

"I had to bring this one. It is different. It is perfect, just perfect, I wanted so much for you to have it." She bit her lip, the tang of blood bloomed over her tongue. "Please," she urged.

"Alright." He reached out. White moonlight fell over his face, turning him white as he buried his teeth into the fruit. He chewed.

The witch thought she would burst with the sight. The door shuddered open. Erzsébet stood within the frame, her hair tousled around her like spun shadow. She glanced at Ficzkó.

"Just a quick visit." He swallowed, and explained, "Dory takes good care of me." He held up the apple.

Erzsébet looked through her lashes, a smile turning her lips. "Oh yes. The witch brings fine gifts."

My lady. So beautiful, so perfect.

The noble girl strode past, lying on the bed. She stretched like a cat before entwining herself about him, her lips found the edge of the fruit. The surprise at seeing her so intimate, so familiar, froze the witch, and she didn't warn her ladyship, didn't pull her away. It wouldn't matter anyway. Their lips touched, the juice of the fruit running down her chin. Ficzkó collapsed into her eagerly.

Fire erupted in the witch's chest, not the burn of desire, but of fury. She burned like a scorned wife, withered like the forgotten dried fruit on the windowsill. She burned and burned and burned and burned until she burst into flames.

—

The girl, Mirella, had stumbled through the woods. Her pretty hair tumbled around her face in coils of distress, as good as blind out there. The woods belonged to the witch's kind, the forgotten and ugly, not to beautiful maids.

The witch bounded forward and threw her body at the maid with all the yearning and desire she'd felt all her life. They fell into the creek and Mirella pummeled with her fists, desperate and aimless. Opaque flickers thickened the witch's mind, which filled with half-remembered naked ankles and mocking whispers. The gathering shadows of a million flies. She shoved Mirella's face under the water.

The maid flailed under the witch's fingers. Lungs shocked by water-filled gasps. The witch pushed Mirella's head until it pressed against the rocks of the shallow bed.

The girl had never really been alive. The beautiful ones rarely lived. Instead they fleshed themselves with worship. Begged for devotions.

He calls me Dory.

Ficzkó liked Mirella too. Worshipped.

The girl's eyes grew empty, like the marbled cuts in a statue of the Roman Venus. Now, Mirella could finally be worthy of devotions. Before, she was a painting that twisted and grunted, pissed and ate. Now, she became art. Quiet and pale, like snow in moonlight. The witch let go.

Mirella bobbed up, white lifeless lips titled into the air. The sight drew an ache from within the witch. She reached down and kissed those cold lips tenderly.

—

Both Ficzkó and Erzsébet lay still, only their chests rising and falling in deep sleep.

The witch wept.

Ugly. So Ugly.

The dancing girls stirred, making her gown quiver.

Why couldn't he see? Why didn't he realize that she loved him more than anyone? Only her. His Dory.

Ugly.

Who saved him when he would have surely died from fever?

Horrid.

The witch crawled over the unconscious pair, putting a miserable head on his chest.

Deep inside her, something snapped, strained for so long, beyond all possible suppleness, a final sickening break, like the trees that broke her mother's body, cracking bones and pushing off the rotted exterior.

A melody played in the faint undercurrents of wind and dust. The old man stroked her hair, blue fingers wiping away tears.

They all owe you.

The medicines, the poison. For cleaned linens and endless ridicule.

Ficzkó owed her.

No one would love him like she did. Why couldn't he see?

Show him. Take what isn't given.

The witch pulled back the covers, kissing him, tasting the salt of his lips and her tears. Erzsébet had unknowingly made him ready for the witch . . . for *his* Dory, ready for her to take the measure of what she had always wanted.

She settled herself over him, bearing down, letting him burst into her center. She rocked and moaned in pleasure and pain. Neither he nor Erzsébet stirred as the witch worked, as she wept over the rage and ecstasy that mounted within her, the blossoms over the pointed white breasts of Mirella, soon to decay. The witch's hands on her throat.

But she had no tears for mother when she remembered the poison, how it wasted her away slowly and painfully. No tears at all. The witch could still see her hateful eyes.

The witch moved forward, gazing upon Erzsébet's perfect face. Heat rose high within her, and the wave of tension broke, filling her with elation. She took what she wanted. Rules for women like the witch had to be rewritten.

Good, good.

If the witch could not have Ficzkó's love, she would have what she could take from him.

This.

And one more thing.

—

The river tinkled like a bell in the darkness, long grasses brushed past his boots in protest of his passing. Agoston made his way to the meeting place. As the moon rose, full and high in the sky, it cast a ghostly glow on pale tree trunks, lighting their spindly naked branches like wraiths reaching for him. The river always seemed otherworldly to him, as if the stories of spirits were not far and all those childhood stories warned of true dangers.

Agoston shook himself. Getting worked up over nothing. It was water. It was night. Night meant darkness—an ideal time to slip away from prying eyes.

His heart beat faster when he thought of Susanna. A fragile woman, not a flower or glass, but like a rusted sword overused and ready to snap. Her kindness drew him, as did the sense that she needed him. The feeling gave him meaning, a meaning he'd searched for at the bottom of wine cups for too long. He chewed a fingernail and spit out the torn remnants.

Where was she?

She would come, she said, her brother with her. Agoston sensed something wrong when she mentioned this brother, sensed that the man's presence would cause him grief. But he went along just the same.

"We'll need to carry him, if he won't leave willingly," Susanna had said.

"If he doesn't want to leave, why take him?"

"I have to."

I have to.

The lack of explanation irritated him, especially with the already existing unease in his stomach. He could go now, right back to his little shop and pretend he hadn't come at all. Pretend he had never met a woman named Susanna who needed help. He'd certainly met prettier women, younger women.

But his feet remained rooted, his body acknowledged what his soul already knew. He wanted to help her, to explain to her they were the same—lost and confused and looking for a new start. They both lived with loneliness that permeated their souls. They could fight that loneliness, together, build a new life, a family. There would be laughter and warmth. The loneliness could never pierce them again.

The river changed its tone to a gurgle and the nighttime sounds dimmed. Something pale reflected the moonlight in the water, floated slowly, bumping against the narrow bank before getting caught in a tiny island of shallow reeds. He moved closer, putting his bag down, and bent toward the water, resisting the urge to light the lantern he had brought lest it give him away to the wrong observers. Forced to creep down a small hill, he stepped cautiously to avoid saturating his boots in an unexpected boggy spot. Clouds moved away from the moon and, as if lit from heaven, illuminated something he recognized. Someone he knew. The innkeeper's daughter. A chill went through him.

Dead.

She wore a white country dress, layers of frills and ribbons floated around her like eels. The fine embroidered flowers decorated the bodice and, more than that, words snaked across the front, stealing Agoston's breath.

Sewn into the front by an unsteady hand were words.

Make me perfect.

34

"Where were the dead girls buried?" He asked again and again, as if he hadn't already heard the answer.

"Everywhere," she said. "Wheat shafts, or left in chambers. Oh dear, has anyone fed them?"

They did that, brought food to their pens, long after the girls had expired.

—

The underbelly of the Nádasdy castle was half brick and half stone with small storage chambers off a large byway. The witch had given clear instructions for their meeting, insisting that it provided her a good cover and reasonable excuse for the use of a wheelbarrow. Susanna had to agree, but she disliked it all the same. A forlorn echo of dripping water greeted her, marking time, maddeningly, as she waited. Her stiff fingers wrapped tightly around the little cross.

So close, she could taste the hope of the world outside the castle walls, Agoston's arms. He'd wait for her. The witch would come through.

Susanna clung to the sputtering lantern and whispered prayers against the damp darkness. If Erszébet found out their plan, there were worse things than castle basements. She drew a shuddering breath. Once she and Ficzkó were out of Sárvár and into the woods, she'd feel better.

Soft scratching and the scuttle of rat feet moved just beyond the lantern's reach. Hopefully, the light would keep them at bay for a little while longer. She hadn't expected the stench here, the sweet smell of rot that made her teeth ache, maybe dead rats or forgotten vegetables.

The moon sat high by now. Perhaps Erszébet had found out, or the witch's plan hadn't worked. Maybe Ficzkó weighed too much for the witch to carry. Susanna shook her head. She'd seen the witch heft water heavier than him. She'd come through. She had to.

Something pale reflected the lamp light, disappearing into a chamber. The soft chime of delicate metal echoed off the walls. It made her think of Erszébet, jeweled and well-corseted for a feast. Susanna's feet shuffled forward, finding shallow puddles. She lifted her lantern higher, trying to ascertain which chamber. A group of rats scattered with a chorus of angry squeals. The smell of rot burst over her like a ruptured boil and she gagged hard enough to steal her breath and well tears in her eyes.

"I'm here," a familiar voice said. "Are you ready?"

Susanna turned but she slipped on the damp floor. The lantern tumbled before her, sputtering and lighting a corpse teeming with rats, soft blonde hair and bloated, gnawed flesh. Its midsection gaped, a cavity of empty organs and messy entrails. Susanna screamed and looked up.

The witch stood over her. For once, the ugly woman's face brought comfort. "Look." Susanna pointed to the moving mass of rats. The oil burned low and so did the flame, turning everything into gray shapes.

The witch nodded. "Rats? Of course."

Susanna's mind rolled, trying desperately to make sense of what she had just seen. An odd note sounded high in the witch's voice. *Run away.*

"Do you have Ficzkó?" Susanna pushed herself up, trembling and breathing hard.

The witch brought the wheelbarrow covered with a canvas, its contents lumpy and shadowed.

"Come take a look." The witch smiled. The shadows lengthened the corners of her mouth until they reached the pits of her eyes.

A wave of loathing rolled over Susanna and she hated depending on this ugly creature, even if the witch loved her brother. God, the smell here, they needed to go. The witch pulled at the corner of the cloth, revealing the contents of the wheelbarrow.

Susanna's stomach dropped. "Is this a trick?"

The wheelbarrow was filled with apples, their skin black in the lantern light.

"Where is Ficzkó?" Susanna demanded. "Where is my brother?" She shouted, her voice hurried and frantic in her own ears, but she couldn't control it. She couldn't control anything at all.

The witch pulled a blade from her skirts. Lantern flames flickered over her sick features. The blue devil stood behind her, his tongue flicking and reaching for Susanna. She screamed.

The blade slashed Susanna's torso, arms, face, a million lacerations. She couldn't breathe. Blood bubbled at her lips, her insides taut and searing. She fell against the wheelbarrow. Apples rolled and scattered.

The rats dispersed in panic, leaving behind something that had been a girl at one time, but was now something stripped of life, of hope, and of flesh. Soon, Susanna would be like her and the rats would have her too. She would finally have her son again.

The witch thrusted and twisted and brought her blade up through Susanna's stomach. She could only gurgle, desperately fighting for air. She lay and choked and shook. The witch worked with mad glee.

The devil peered close, face to face, tasting Susanna's suffering.

And then.

Nothing.

PART IV
HAPPILY EVER AFTER

35

January 1588

Agoston picked up a block of wood, mindlessly whittling as he spoke, his fingers needing the distraction of busyness. "It is time the two of you knew" he said. "Fourteen years is near grown-up and my heart can't handle keeping it from you any longer." He proceeded to tell his two adopted daughters a story about a man whose corpse decorated the walls of Sárvár castle.

The man had been a castle guard, rumored to have personally offended Count Nádasdy, and he was tortured for insolence. When, finally, the man hung over the wall with his intestines dangling from a split belly, the wind used his pain to throw red designs against the whitewash. Father told the story as a warning. A reminder, that those who live within the castle are fickle beings. Like gods, they required sacrifice and worship. But even that, at times, wouldn't be enough to satisfy them. And the events of the story, he told them, happened the year he took them in, Anna and Nusi, two motherless newborns.

"The knock came late in the night," Agoston said. "Opened the door to find a castle servant holding two angels fast asleep in their swaddling. Little did I know how much they would wail." He laughed.

"Did the servant say who our mothers were?" Anna asked. Recently, a hunger had grown within her to know herself, to know where she came from.

Agoston grew serious. "She said I was to keep things secret. That you both were bastard born and one of you was the child of the countess herself. And that man on the wall. Well, he'd been the father."

Anna clasped Nusi's hand.

"Thank you"—Nusi put a hand on Agoston's arm—"for telling us."

Anna said nothing, but her heart swirled with possibilities. A daughter of the countess? Which of them could be the bastard offspring of a noblewoman? And if they had different mothers, why did they look like the sisters they claimed they were? The image of the hanged man from her father's story loomed in her mind, more questions, and fear.

—

Neither girl could sleep that night, tossing and turning in the bed they shared.

"Do you think it's true?" Nusi asked. "That we are noblewomen?"

Anna smacked her. "Has father ever lied?"

Nusi rolled to her side and propped her chin on her hand. "I'm going up there."

Anna sat up, the hair on her arms prickling like spikes. "What?" She almost shouted. "No you're not."

"Yes, I am."

"You won't come back," said Anna. "No one comes back."

"That servant woman did and with us on top of that. What if I find our mothers? I've got to try." Nusi sighed.

"What if you don't?"

"Don't what? Find them?"

"No." Anna gulped, and then said, "Come back."

Nusi paused for a moment and chewed her lip, a habit she developed when confronted with a problem. She rarely took long to solve them, and this was no exception. "Then you can have my dresses," she said.

"I'm not you." Anna's voice tumbled but she wanted to scream, to kick off the blankets, to talk plainly and honestly.

Nusi snuggled close, protectively stroking Anna's hair. "No, you're not. You're you."

When morning came, Anna thought that, maybe, if she lounged in bed and faked illness, that Nusi would stay—a foolish hope. In the end, Nusi left, alone, into the chill morning. When Anna finally rushed to the door, she saw only the last swish of her sister's long black hair as she rounded the pathway into the hills.

36

Autumn, 1590

Within the castle kitchens, a girl carefully stuffed the smallest portions of bread between the spaces of thread and swollen flesh of her tightly sewn lips. The maid winced with every effort, bringing fresh wells of blood through crusted bruises. She must be so very hungry. The thought caused the witch to grin, the corners of her lips pulling over the awkward protrusion of teeth.

Any girl who caught Count Ferenc's eye was punished. Ruined. In the world of the Countess Erszébet Báthory, only she could exist as the fairest. The witch saved some, plucked them before the countess could ruin them. She made them perfect and kept them safe.

Of course, she couldn't save them all.

The girl muffled a groan behind her tightly closed lips, still a pretty thing despite the recent adjustments. Her long dark hair spilled in alluring disarray. Too bad her ladyship had marred the girl before the witch could have her. The countess would be sure to sew those lips tighter and tighter until they became the most natural fusion of flesh, until the girl withered and disappeared entirely from lack of food and water. Perhaps, she would try to stuff the bread up her nose, like the last girl.

The witch stepped into the dim perimeter of the candlelight. "Don't let the countess find you, Nusi."

158

The countess, the beautiful countess, the hungry woman of Sárvár. Not like this girl, who had only felt the hunger of the body, but one who hungered all her life.

The witch's hands darted toward the maid's face, all sharp angles of suffering.

Beautiful. So beautiful.

This jarred the maid into motion, her thick lashes almost touching her eyebrows with fear. Picking up her skirts, she dashed from the kitchen with a shadowy jostle of cleavage.

The witch filled with regret. Her hands longed to sew and decorate. To cut behind the breasts and pack her insides with the sweet scent of lavender. The old man muttered from the dark corners. The witch could barely remember what came before Sárvár. What her mind sounded like without the voice of the old man and all the others. Always calling to her. Before the dancing girls had draped themselves over her, clothing her in beauty and song. The witch moved to gather butchering knives.

The cadence of existence within the castle revolved less around the shortening and lengthening of days, but of military campaigns. Ottoman incursions, news of victories and defeats, all marked the waxing and waning of life. When the count returned home, to attempt to plant a new child in his wife and plan his next campaign, no matter the time of year, the castle turned warm and the countess mellowed. Until, of course, the pretty maids milled to and fro the count's quarters. Then, the dark clouds gathered within the countess's burning eyes and over Sárvár castle. And rivers ran scarlet with the blood of girls.

—

Ficzkó sauntered into the village with swagger. He had come to enjoy the vestments of loaned power. It didn't give him everything he wanted, but it certainly gave him advantage. Wherever his sister had gone, she'd be shocked to see him now. Perhaps he'd still find her, out in some hovel and she'd beg for him to save her. He sneered and a surge of familiar anger came over him, followed by hot shame. Good that she did not see him, and what he did now.

He'd been to this village some time ago, in the early days after Susanna disappeared. Not long after, the countess directed his new vocation, searching out serving maids for the ever short-staffed castle. He guided his horse to where he remembered an inn stood, ready to get out of the chill shadows of dusk. Eager to fill a cup with something to burn away the guilt.

He didn't exactly know what Erszébet did with the cargo he brought to her, but he heard their screams. Sometimes, he stuffed his ears and hated himself, yet he returned again and again, doing as she bid. At first, it was because she had carried his child. After the child had been whisked away to someplace he'd never know, his body moved like the puppet Erszébet had made of him.

Susanna had left him behind. She threw him away like he didn't matter, like he hadn't spent all those years caring for her, watching out for her. The old pain settled into his flesh, turning to acid. He let out a hot breath and narrowed his eyes. He had a job to do.

Inside the inn, a small common room rolled out before him, mostly empty besides a pair of farmers who mulled over their wine by the fire. Ficzkó shook his cloak, welcoming the warmth and revealing the embroidered Báthory-Nádasdy crest, careful to keep it draped over the shoulder that ended in nothingness. He didn't mind his deformity, but had found it best to make connections first so people saw him as whole before focusing on what he lacked.

"Welcome, welcome," the innkeeper called out, bustling him to a seat near the fire. A smiled fixed on her face, the middle-aged woman hurried back to the kitchen in a puff of brittle hair. Soon, a plate of fried dough and thick slices of sausage followed and the long-awaited cup of wine. Ficzkó drank it down appreciatively.

"What has brought you to Völcsej?" she said, her accent like a gaggle of birds.

He took a bite of the dough and didn't look up, chewing thoughtfully. "I am looking to hire maidservants for the Countess Báthory." Usually, such statements were met with contained excitement this far from Sárvár. The closer to the seat of Nádasdy power, parents hid their daughters. Like him, no one fully knew what happened to those servants, but they knew they did not return.

"Is that right?" The innkeeper's eyes glittered, that stupid smile widened as if the corners of her mouth reached for her earlobes.

Völcsej, just one of many small towns and villages on the edge of the Habsburg world and far enough, it seemed.

"Any girls looking for work here?" Ficzkó asked.

"Always someone looking for work and those who weren't, they just didn't know they were." She refilled his cup. "Serving with a noble lady, lots of girls who'd jump at that offer."

Another farmer had joined the fire. Streaks of dirt still littered his face and he wiped his hands on his shirt before embracing his friend. Snatches of conversation about the harvest floated to Ficzkó, but his gaze had settled on the girl who had pushed herself into a corner, picking at her skirts.

He smiled. His journey would be a short one this time. He had found her.

A bloom at the cusp of womanhood, wisps of honey hair escaping the gathered binding of a red handkerchief. He desired her, just like the others he had brought to the countess. Girls such as her had little interest in men of his age, especially one-armed men. He no longer had the tint of distinguished manhood to help him past the missing limb. Instead, he had edged too close to old age for attraction.

The guilt melted into lust, as it always did. It made him eager to do his work and to claim his reward.

37

Anna hadn't the heart to tell father where she headed. Instead, she packed lightly and slipped out as the sun rose, toward the castle, the same way her sister had the year before. She bounded along the path, her breath clouding before her, with a confidence she did not feel. Sometimes, hope could be enough to drive things forward. A small inner voice warned that she ventured toward disaster. Yet she strode forward, forcing herself to dwell on good things.

Work in a castle brought payment, money she could give to her father, perhaps even a little for dresses of her own. Perhaps she'd find her sister, happy in the castle, doing well with a new family and light in her eyes. Then, she'd find her mother, who had wanted her all along and been parted from her daughter unjustly. Her mother would take one look and know she had a daughter.

Anna's footsteps quickened, the sunrise lighting the hills and clusters of naked trees with orange. The castle came within view, its roofs in red, looming over the pale flesh of its towers. Windows stared like empty sockets, casting about for light they remembered but could no longer sense. She suppressed a shiver and clutched her skirts. Nusi's skirts. As the towers grew larger, the sound of a horse clattered from behind and Anna twirled to look.

"Good morning, girl," Ficzkó called, "where might you be going?"

His voice was friendly and contained a lilt of joviality. A young girl saddled behind him and peeked out at Anna with wide eyes. Ficzkó dressed in simple but quality cloth, the steed well groomed. Anna cast her eyes down, a habit she had forced herself to develop, as men did not like women looking at them too boldly. Yet the action fed a core of anger with her each time she did it.

"Good morning, sir."

"Bah, don't call me that, and look up, you can't see where you're going without looking around."

The comment made Anna smile and a sort of relief flowed over her.

"You're heading toward the castle, if you don't know it. Just in case you were looking down while walking along." Ficzkó brought his horse to a stop. The girl behind him continued to stare, strands of her blonde hair escaping the red handkerchief she wore over her head.

"I mean to go there," Anna said. "Looking to find work serving the house."

"What luck," Ficzkó said.

"Pardon me?"

The girl on the horse laid her head on the man's back and closed her eyes, like a resting child.

"Difficult to find good serving staff these days," he said, a grin making his wiry whiskers stick out in opposing directions. "I happen to be hiring maidservants at the direction of the Lady Báthory. As you can see, I've only returned with one."

Excitement lumped in Anna's middle. "Truly?"

He laughed. "I'll be happy to make that two, if you'd oblige me. Plus, it'll make me seem much more successful in my venture."

"Yes, I'd like that."

"Wonderful then, we are mere steps away," he said. "I can get us through the gate."

———

The witch opened the door to the countess's receiving rooms, letting the golden glow of the fire wash over the tension that had developed in her shoulders. A young woman dallied lazily on the large rug before the fire, chasing away the chill. As the witch entered, the woman gazed in veiled revulsion. Words without the movement of lips, the woman didn't know that she begged, a soul asking the witch without motioning her hands.

Make me beautiful.

Not a maidservant, the witch realized suddenly. The dress too clean and well-cut, no patches or rips. A noble, though not highborn, probably from one of the lesser nobles that dallied on the edge between the lands of the emperor and Royal Hungary, but a noble nonetheless. A thrill passed through the witch, she had never cut a noble before.

"Dory." Erszébet glowed from a chair by the fire, her proud Báthory forehead made more prominent by the high gathering of her dark hair, woven with velvet ribbon. On each earlobe a garnet in the shape of a tear swung like suspended blood drops. "I've been waiting."

"My lady," the witch said, glancing about.

Erszébet's face pinched hungrily, running her fingers through soft ringlets of the woman's hair. Eyes drooping, half lidded, a drink fell from the woman's limp hand. The witch smiled, the hunger rose in her too.

She could always could hear the souls of these beauties at the crucial moment, asking forever for the perfection they craved, sense how flesh tightened over bones, taste their liquid desire of men, the rippling of the supple youthful muscles. Erszébet would claim this girl like she did many others, then, ruin them. A sad waste, but only a select few were destined for the witch's keeping and she chose them carefully and well.

Erszébet bound the young woman's hands as the witch pulled at the rope that dropped from the ceiling in a series of rings. She grunted a little, finally bringing the woman off the ground, her feet dangling just like those earrings. A maid, the one with the sewn mouth brought a large metal bowl, sliding it under the woman's feet. Erszébet already had one of the kitchen blades, watching her own reflection in the metal. The woman mouthed wordlessly, her head lolling to one side.

The witch cocked her ear, bringing it closer to hear. No sound, the woman's lips no longer moved. Yet the witch heard her. They always spoke to her like this. It's how she knew they were the perfect ones. The difference between rage and art.

Make me beautiful. The words came, but not from the young woman. They echoed from outside the room, outside the castle. *Make me beautiful.* Not this woman. Another, just beyond. Approaching, drawn and calling to the witch. This woman hanging here belonged only to Erszébet.

Opening her dark, honey eyes, the woman tried to bring the witch into focus in a world becoming increasingly hazy. Her lips curled a sultry pout of welcome, an invitation. As if the witch played the suitor.

Her ladyship readied the blade, breathing heavily, heat licking like flames from her eyes. Destruction and ruin. Like all the rest, Erszébet said, "White as snow, white as snow, white as . . ."

———

The soulful look of Anna's eyes, and the soft flutter over her lips, twisted Ficzkó's heart. He could tell himself that the dark-haired beauty changed him, just by her presence. But, no, these things would be lies. He had not changed. Instead, he saw another peering from those eyes like a memory reborn. He saw Susanna.

How or why, Ficzkó couldn't figure, they held no significant semblance to one another, but how the girl moved, as if she held the weight of the world on her shoulders . . . so he brought the girl, Anna, to Ilona. Leaving her in the washroom would hide her for some time. Protect the girl from the eyes of the countess. He'd like to talk with her more, know her.

With a sigh, Ficzkó brought his first catch, the farmer's daughter, to an empty bedroll in what appeared as servant's quarters. He'd done this many times before to the unsuspecting. Several of these bedrolls had popped up throughout the castle, as the countess discouraged the use of the hall, except when the count returned to residence. Communal living led to discussions and these of course led to the passing of rumors, things better controlled.

The girl clung to him, anxiety overtaking her. "Please, sir," she said, and casted a glance at the whitewashed walls, a towering sense of enclosure she'd likely never experienced before. Never mind what he'd done to her on the road, in this world, she knew no one but him. The control thrilled him for a moment, but he couldn't enjoy it. Memories of Susanna haunted him.

He could do it right now, lose himself in this girl's flesh again. She'd fight less now. They usually did after the first time, as if they had already begun to die. He didn't look at her. "Rest while you can. The countess will require your services soon enough."

He left her and stalked to his own quarters, the same forgotten room Erszébet had installed him in so many years ago. The door shut behind him and he sat, trying desperately to remember the last time he saw Susanna. He could almost see her here, her eyes swollen with tears, holding a tiny wooden cross.

The night she'd disappeared, he'd been with Erszébet. Intoxicated on the forbidden. Sometimes, when he tried to recall that night, he found holes in his memory, like black spots. The witch, Dory, stared back at him from the darkness.

"I thought you'd never wake up," Susanna had said, standing right there on the other side of this room.

Ficzkó scrubbed a hand through his hair. Had he woken up? How did he get here? How did he become this? When had he made these choices? How much choice did he really have? He and the farmer girl suddenly had much in common. Their lives, offered to those who held control, on an altar of their own making.

Ferenc had returned from war to find his betrothed's belly growing with a child he had not planted. The man's rage howled from one end of the castle to the other. Ficzkó hid in this room, sure he'd be discovered as the father. Erszébet no longer came to see him. Susanna had abandoned him.

When Ficzkó finally became brave enough to return to Ilona for work, he watched the count string up a soldier named Janos. The man died screaming as he hung, the contents of his belly swinging in the wind. For weeks, Ficzkó passed the sickening display. The man had been named as the commoner who had dared to father a child on the future countess.

And he watched as the witch's belly seemed to grow in mockery of Erszébet's and the sight of it made Ficzkó shiver, as if feverish again. So, when Erszébet tasked him with errands beyond the castle, he took up the work eagerly. If he opened his window now, he could look out upon the spot the man's body had hung, and almost see an outline of him there. The shape was of Ficzkó's own guilt and the truth of his powerlessness. Worse, how he did not wish for change.

38

"Witnesses say there was a girl, a wash maid? Who was she?"
The inquisitor had stumbled on the one question that could not
be answered with truth and it gave him power. The chair rocked
back and forth, pounding at the dusty stone floor. The world
smelled of char and white pretty flowers.

There were two.

Two.

60.

"I can't remember," she said.

—

The castle was cold, not from the weather, but from something
intangible, as if the structure beat an endless frozen river, its
veins creeping through the whitewash, worming into bedposts
and hearths until there could only be coming death. The end of
everything. Anna shivered in the hall where she made her bed,
shivered more as she scrubbed clothes in frigid water.

There were few people to talk to, mostly just fine furniture and
grand tapestries, paintings and vases. Sometimes, the emptiness
overwhelmed, time echoing off the walls. Guards stayed to
military matters, practiced in the courtyard, eating, rotating
patrols and sleeping in their barracks. What servants around were

few, mostly deformed or sturdy old women and mature men. No sign of her sister. It was as if she never existed. Anna began to doubt, that perhaps her sister had not come here after all. Perhaps she simply decided to go elsewhere for work, maybe something happened to her.

Maybe the castle happened to her.

The stray thought gave her a new chill.

Ilona knew each small group of servants by name, her gravelly voice strong and curt, issuing jobs for the day, meals, chores, projects for the upkeep of whitewash and repairs. There were not enough of them, so work mounted at an unbearable pace, constant and overwhelming. Anna had been stationed as the sole laundress, the previous one, having gone to work as a personal servant to the countess. No one named the girl, or talked further about her. When Anna dared to ask Ilona, she found only a hostile glare and an order to get back to work as her answer.

"Hey," a woman called.

Anna turned, startled at the break of silence, her fingers numb from washing. A maidservant watched her curiously from the hall, her face a pathway of scarred lines, crisscrossing along cheeks, over her nose and forehead, finally nestling into her tightly bound hair.

"You look familiar," she said, switching a basket of dirty linens from one hip to the other.

Anna's heart fluttered.

"Have you been to the castle before?" she continued, a thoughtful look on her scarred face. "I've worked here for a long time. Seen many come and"—she paused and a shadowed flickered over her features—"and go."

Anna licked her lips. "I've never been here before."

The woman nodded, then suddenly smiled, cheerful enough that it broke through the lines of her scars, but not full enough to reach the sadness of her eyes. "Must be remembering wrong. Bah. I'm Reka," she said. "So glad we have a laundress again."

Silence fell between them like a waterfall. The woman looked as if she wanted to say something more.

"Thank you," Anna said, and moved to take the load from her. "It's nice to meet you. I'm Anna."

The maid paused.

Most people spent their lives working on masks to hide their authentic selves from the world. But Anna had been born with one she didn't know how to remove. She knew a lot about hiding the truth, how to veil the eyes, to look away when fear struck. She could see it like a hawk tracking a mouse. She squared her shoulders and cleared her throat. "What is it?"

Reka averted her gaze. "I'm sorry, I didn't mean to stare."

Anna nodded, patient, waiting.

Reka shifted, the scars on her face suddenly lying flat and placid. "You look like someone. Someone who worked here." She motioned to the washroom.

Anna's blood pulsed loud in her ears. "How long ago? Where is that person now?"

"Several seasons ago. It all melds together." Reka put a hand to her temple. "I don't know where she is. She disappeared. They all disappear after a while. You will too." She looked up bleakly. "And if they ever reappear, you'll wish that they hadn't."

"Is that what happened?" Anna asked, motioning gently to the scars of Reka's face.

The woman put a hand to a cheek as if she had forgotten. "No, I did this. I did this so I would not be one of them. I can't leave. I . . . I have a son here. We all know that it is the pretty ones that disappear."

"I'm looking for my sister. She came to the castle for work three years ago. She looks like me." Anna beat down the edge of panic, the urgency for information, for everything this woman knew. "Where do they go? What happens to them?" Words tumbled out, belying her anxiety, urged on by the look of terror and sorrow in Reka's eyes, a sense that this woman might understand, might help.

"I . . ." Reka stammered. "I don't know." Her eyes darted and she lowered her voice. "But you should leave while you can. It's only a matter a time."

"I have to find my sister," Anna said. *And my mother,* she intoned silently.

The washroom door opened. Ilona locked her gaze on the two, standing awkwardly with piles of soiled linens between them. "There isn't time for standing about idle. Get working," she barked. A set of keys jangled on her hip.

Reka curtsied and twirled away, her demeanor still girl-like. Anna looked after her for a moment before she gathered the linens and cast her hands back into the frigid water.

———

No one talked about the girls who disappeared. There weren't many servants left to talk anyhow. The ones who could have talked, Lady Báthory had a way of making them not able to.

Reka came to a small door, the kind that hid crevices throughout the castle for use of storage. There were many of these chambers scattered around the castle. She cracked it and crawled through, shutting the door behind her. Colorless light filtered through a crack, giving the small space an ethereal look. The familiar arms of her son swung around her neck and Reka pulled him to her, breathing in his familiar scent. He was growing so fast, ten winters soon.

A figure hunched in the corner, thin and haggard.

"How is she?" Reka asked, meeting the dark eyes of her child.

"She moaned a bit through the night, but no worse than the first night. I've been able to get her to drink a little watered wine through a small opening."

"Good. You've done well."

Reka scooted closer to the huddled creature. The girl's lips seeped and swelled around black stitching. "Let me cut the threads, it will hurt, but it will heal and you can eat."

The girl recoiled. Fear passed over her eyes. She tried to meld into the stone behind her.

"Shhhh. There, it's alright. I won't do it then." Reka held her hands up, to show her goodwill.

"I need to tell you something." Reka took a deep breath and looked at her son. "Get to your work, Pál."

"But I—"

"Go before they begin to search for you."

Pál hung his head. "Yes, alright."

The satisfying click of the small door closing brought Reka back to the task at hand. "There is a new maid."

The girl's eyes flashed.

"She looks like you." Reka poured wine into a cup, carefully diluting it with water. She pushed the tiniest crust of bread into the solution, breaking it up, turning the liquid into a thin gruel. She looked into the girl's eyes, dark saucers of intense awareness. She had frozen. "She says she's your sister."

Tears spilled over the girl's dirty cheeks.

"She is, isn't she?"

The girl stared at the twisted ruin of her feet.

"She's here to find you."

Reka took a tiny spoon and held it out, offering some of the gruel. "Eat."

The girl shook her head, hair hanging limp, lice weaving themselves around her scalp.

"You'll need your strength." Reka urged the spoon forward again.

The poor maid pushed it away, the exertion leaving her visibly shaking.

Reka let her arms drop. She understood. Either the girl would die here or at the hands of the countess. Better to starve than die butchered.

39

News of the Count Ferenc's impending arrival reached Sárvár at the same time as the gathering of heavy dark clouds on the horizon. A deep cold had set in, piercing the walls. Guards and servants clutched cloaks and draped blankets over themselves as they attempted to make the castle ready.

"Bringing refugees with him," Ilona explained. "Just more fodder to wait on the nobles if you ask me."

Anna stoked the fire, keeping it hot enough to allow the washing to dry instead of freeze. "All the servants seem scared."

Ilona threw a look over her nose. "Right they are. Countess gets mean when the lord returns. More mean than usual." She pressed her lips together into a straight line. "Never mind all that. Finish up the load, there's more to do after."

Outside, the wind howled through the vacant spaces, whipping around corners like death itself. Anna fished linens from the water, hanging them carefully on lines strung throughout the washroom. Even here, the chill created drafts that made Anna shiver. Just as soon as she had finished, Ilona pushed a basket of clean shirts and breeches. "Deliver these to the stable."

Wrapping a shawl around herself, Anna entered the courtyard. A wet snow fell from the black sky, so heavy that the wind barely had an effect on its descent. As each flake met the ground, they seemed to splatter and freeze, threatening to coat the world in ice. Guards scowled at the sky and each other as they made their rounds. No one else seemed about. The gate remained as sealed as ever.

A series of torches had been lit in the stables, giving some light and welcome warmth. "Hullo?" Anna called. "I've come with the wash."

A hand pulled her into a nearby stall.

"Shhhhh, it's just me."

Anna looked up to see Reka's scarred face, a younger boy by her side. Reka gripped Anna, clung to her hand with a silent desperation. The boy sunk back into the confines of the stable as if the hay would hide him.

"I know where your sister is," Reka said.

Anna sucked in air. "My sister? Where? Where is she?"

"Keep your voice down," Reka said. "I'm offering you a deal, okay, do you understand?"

Anna nodded, still trying to shake off the shock.

"Good." Reka ushered the boy into the light, a helpless youth, but old enough to understand his helplessness. "I will help you find your sister. But when you do, promise me you will leave and take my son with you."

"Yes," Anna said.

"Say it," Reka urged, "say that you'll promise."

Anna's mouth went dry, making it hard to form words, but she forced her lips and tongue to work. "If you help me, I promise to leave and take your son with me."

Reka breathed heavy, as if the extraction of those words was a physical labor. She stumbled a few steps backward, the scars on her face a map of streams and rivers joining and splitting. The boy reached up and gripped her hand.

"I don't want to leave you," he said.

Reka went to her knees, her eyes pools of sorrow and dedication. "I know," she said, putting a hand to the boy's cheek. "I know."

Anna shivered and fought the urge to pass out. A creeping sensation went up her back, folding into her spine. She watched the boy try to restrain the tears in his eyes.

"Why don't you try to escape with him?" Anna said.

"If the count finds out I'm missing—he knows I'd never leave Pál behind. He'll have us hunted. But if I'm still here, he won't know yet. It will buy time."

Anna put down the basket in confusion. "But why would he care? He's not even here now."

Drawing a ragged breath, Reka licked her lips. "The count has me watched when he's out on campaign." She reddened and put a hand on the boy's shoulder protectively.

Anna realized, motioning toward the boy. "This is the count's son."

Reka nodded. "After the snow passes, I'll bring you to your sister and you'll leave with Pál, alright?"

Anna pursed her lips. "Alright."

40

The storm swirled endlessly. Ice fell from the sky like angry pelts from a giant, taking aim at every surface, transforming the world into frozen sculptures. The east tower had partially crumbled inward, its beams exposed to the air. And then, as if in denial of its previous brutality, nature now fluttered layers of snow.

Ficzkó ached with the cold. His lost arm hated winter most of all, where it remained freezing and painful as if it still existed. He looked up, assessing the tower's damage and he sighed. To repair, he'd need a damned team and the castle had so little help to spare that he'd be forced to hire laborers for the job. The countess would not be happy.

Ilona huffed through the courtyard, her hands twisting together and face pinched. One of the few servants that had lasted any length of time, like him. He'd grown fond of the oak of a woman. He always wondered what she thought happened to the girls he brought the countess, but she never indicated any curiosity on the matter. Maybe, like him, she'd rather not know, it made it easier to go on.

"Count's returning," Ilona explained briskly. "Got a village with him too."

The count. Lord Nádasdy. Ferenc. The Black Captain. Hero of Hungary.

The greatness of Lord Nádasdy made Ficzkó's skin tighten. The count's children were not given away in the dead of the night, taken into the darkness, never to return. Ficzkó had never seen his child, let alone hold it. She'd be a young woman now. The same age as the girls he harvested for Erszébet. A stab to the soul. A thought struck him, that pretty new girl he'd dropped with Ilona... she'd be the right age, wouldn't she? Erszébet had the babe smuggled out and drowned, hadn't she? Ferenc would have settled for no less.

The guards above called and answered. Only now did Ficzkó hear the shuffle of horses beyond the gate, the portcullis being lifted with a squeal of protest to the wet and the cold.

The count.

Ficzkó threw another glance at the damaged tower and grunted to himself. The poor man who'd been gutted and left as a warning had hung on the wall just below that tower, his insides a feast for the birds. A guard had unfurled Nádasdy and Báthory banners over the spot today. The only birds there now were painted on the Nádasdy crest it. That was the way of Hungary, new proud paint over old horrendous blood. The Habsburgs had no idea what they had gotten themselves into. The thought made him chuckle.

If the count knew the truth, it would be Ficzkó on that wall. His heart fluttered, gritting his teeth, he forced himself to look away. Trying to remember those times when he had the arrogance to take a noblewoman in his bed. Yet pieces of those memories ran away from him and the witch's repulsive face emerged from the center of the confusion. That night she had visited him and that night Erszébet had followed. An apple. Sweet juice had laced his tongue.

Rumor in the castle claimed it was an apple that killed the old baroness.

Unlike the old lady, he continued to live. Yet memories of the night still escaped him. A feeling of wrongness and discomfort always accompanied his questions. As if something had been taken from him and he could never get it back.

The scant serving staff had begun to filter into the courtyard, ready to receive and welcome the lord back from his travels. Standing in the back, he spotted Anna pushing her curtain of hair from her face. All darkness and cream, old Hungarian blood and restless soulfulness, the lily petals of her skin unmarred, almost as if nothing had ever touched her and he ached to reach out. Just as he had with Susanna. The sudden appearance of Anna sparked these memories, made him dwell on the past more and more. Familiar and alien, comfort and violation—driving him to covet and burn the shame of his misdeeds like incense. As if she held some kind of key to understanding himself and everything. Ficzkó stalked toward her, ignoring the count's arrival.

"Who are you?" He blurted, his usual buttery words leaving him.

She recoiled as if slapped. "Anna," she said simply, letting the name fall like a wave of heat from her lips.

"No. I know your name, but who are you really? Where did you come from?"

"Sárvár." She motioned helplessly.

A cheer went up around them. Shouts of welcome. Answering calls, louder than normal. More voices.

"Your parents?" He pushed, spittle flying from his mouth.

The girl's eyes took on a haunted look. "I don't know," she said, almost too low to hear. "I was abandoned as a babe." She looked away. "I may be the countess's child. A bastard."

Ficzkó chilled. His senses sharpened. His own child. Long lost. His absent hand reached for her. Not love but desire. To covet.

A shadow fell over them. The count watched from his horse, snow dancing around the bearded face. Anna glanced up, her luminous eyes widening. The count stared at her.

The countess's voice rang clear through the courtyard. "Welcome home, my lord. I see you have brought new servants." Her sharp eyes noted her husband's attention, looking from Ferenc to the girl with a chilling smile. Ficzkó knew that smile all too well. Erszébet used it just before she plucked a girl and they'd be gone forever. Gone away, to wherever the place was they all went, screaming.

The count inclined his head toward the girl with a smirk.

Anna curtsied, dark hair falling like water, her young body bending like a willow in the wind.

"Indeed, my lady. And I return from my travels to find a jewel nestled in my castle," the count said.

That itch returned to Ficzkó, his bones restless in his hide, his sins squirming inside him.

Once the count turned his attentions elsewhere, like a dark sun moving to illuminate another corrupt sky, Ficzkó grabbed Anna's shoulder. Urgency ran through him, an electric compulsion. He held her fast, even as she stiffened, trying to pull back. His shadow hand grabbed at her too, curling into itself, desperate to clasp something real. He ignored it. "Go home. Get out of this castle. Leave. You aren't safe here. No one is safe here."

Her mouth slackened and the faint pink sight of her tongue drove a sharp desire. How he wanted to drink her in and spit her out.

"I can't."

Ficzkó released her, almost angry.

"I'm trying to find my sister."

"What?"

"What happens to the girls here? Why is it dangerous?"

Shame gutted him.

"I don't know." That was the truth, right? He remembered how the crook of their arms tightened on his as he led them to Erszébet. Into that deep dark, not even he dared to go. He'd tell himself that the girls would escape. The youngest one, she had been, maybe, ten or eleven winters old.

Had been.

—

Wishing to catch a glimpse of the countess, Anna had believed she could slink quietly behind the servants and watch without drawing attention. How very wrong she was. Ficzkó had dragged her into a doorway. His face pinched and haunted, and his eyes boring into her soul. Fingers dug insistent points of pain on her arm even after he released her. The change in his demeanor startled her, made her mind scatter.

"What do you mean, sister?" he asked.

Anna tried to slow her heart, seeking to explain, to make him stop staring at her. "There were two of us, left as babies. I was told," she gulped, "that our mothers were in the castle, one a servant and the other the countess."

"Look at me," the man demanded, stepping too close.

She tried to squirm away and could have, but something

stopped her. She peered into his feverish face. His nose tilted with a scowl.

"I know you. For the love of god, I know you, girl." He pushed away. "Damn that witch."

Anna thought she saw a shimmer of tears in his eyes. She reached out, but he spun and stalked back into the daylight, disappearing into the crowd.

41

Age leaves people with experience, but it doesn't necessarily leave them with a sense of that experience. Pieces of themselves, littered throughout the timeline of their lives. The witch's pieces dwelt forever at the worst moments of her life. Pieces of her still swam under the trees, skeletons feeding the roots, sprouting spring leaves with decaying flesh. Pieces of her, like the smell of sickness in the cabin by the river. Poisons ingested by her mother, until she had vomited nothing but blood. How the witch boiled death into the broth, spoon fed the woman until she could smell its faint scent on her sickly skin. Mother knew, but too late. She could no longer speak or lift her hands, turn her head or fight the urge to swallow, as her daughter shoved spoonful after spoonful into her gaping, ugly mouth.

Part of the witch still lived back there, still feeding poison, not unlike the hate that the witch had ingested her whole life. Her own twisted face, gaping, she knew there was poison, but she couldn't stop swallowing. She studied the apple in her hand, midnight-red flesh taut over the snowy sweetness it contained. A picture of perfection.

Always a shame to consume it, use it and throw out the core. The witch didn't do that. She saved them, made them better, kept them perfect. Lining a large clearing, she had erected beds of glass sarcophagi for her incorruptible beauties. So many had already been found, their pale placid expressions thanked her in turn, for they were the perfect ones. Forever. But the princess of them all, the one, her glass bed still waited, longing for her arrival, glittering in the torchlight. A wooded courtyard of perfection. They didn't know that the witch had saturated them, owned them, just as mother didn't know, at first. The witch prepared them, drained their bodies of impurity. They begged with the chorus of their voices. Called her.

Make me perfect.

The witch's newest beauty gazed up at her from the bower of snow. Too weak to fight or move, let alone speak. Except the girl's eyes, sometimes, she closed them when the witch approached, to block out the fear. Other times, she watched so closely that she didn't blink. Time came for the witch to have her, to don her like a beautiful gown.

The countess abused, left her girls disfigured, broken and bruised. They died ugly. That's what the countess needed from them, to ruin their beauty like one shreds a painting. As the noblewoman aged, her own famous beauty slowly wilting, she needed the ruin more than ever.

Not the witch. She didn't do that to her girls. She collected them, loved them, and made them better than they could have ever dreamed. The witch's girls were the perfect ones.

Sometimes, she'd pluck one harvested by Ficzkó during his errands for the countess. The witch savored those, pulling their skin over herself like a blanket. She could finally be with him, just as she had so many years before. Their experience became hers, their fear her thrill.

This little farmer girl had been Ficzkó's catch. The witch tingled, anticipating everything, these moments that she lived for. Sipping the substance that would finally give the girl to her, a concoction of mushrooms and herbs, and she straddled her beauty, knife in hand. This time, the girl kept her eyes open. The effects of the drug coursed through the witch's veins as she leaned forward until they met face to face. Need fired through her body and in her mind, she pressed herself harder. The girl's chest rose and fell in short bursts.

The witch flicked her tongue over the girl's lips, enjoying the taste of salt and roses. When she couldn't bear to wait any longer, she pushed her tongue into the girl's mouth, tasted the soft pink within. Then, she sucked out the spirit and pushed the blade through the girl's neck. The beauty's body convulsed, soft subtle tremors, blood welled outward, grabbing at the witch, begging for her. So the witch did as the girl bid, slipped inside her skin and peered through those beautiful, perfect eyes. They were hers, the perfect ones, all hers.

An old familiar voice dragged just beyond her awareness.

See. Didn't I promise you I'd make you beautiful?

42

"Ferenc is returned," the countess said. Her face pinched in the mirror.

"Yes, my lady." Reka pulled the woman's dark hair up, gently twisting and coiling it into place. A few strands of silver stood out, but only Reka noticed them. Those were just now sprouting, but soon enough they'd claim the whole head. The countess would, no doubt, find a girl to beat and torture when she realized.

The woman drummed her fingers on the lacquered desk in front of her. "And yet he still hasn't come to see me."

Reka's fingers twitched, the tips still chill.

"You seem nervous." The countess arched an eyebrow. "Has he called for you?"

Reka shook her head. Ferenc had long stopped calling for her, not since she cut herself. Pushing through one last pin, she stepped back checking over her work. "There your ladyship, you look beautiful."

The mirror reflected all the planes and angles of the countess's face, sweet to look upon still. "I will always be the fairest, you understand that, Reka, don't you? Smart to do what you did."

"Yes, my lady."

The countess's face emptied of color. She stood, pressing a hand to her head. "Who was the girl in the courtyard? The one

Ferenc admired."

"I'm sorry, my lady?" Running out of time, once the countess set her sights on someone, it wouldn't take long before . . . if only this blasted snow would stop. No use sending Pál to die of cold. "I'm not sure." The lie came thick to her tongue.

The countess's eyes answered with fire and she pressed a small bottle to her lips. She lay back on the coverlets of her bed, crushing the coils of hair Reka had so carefully fixed. Another headache.

"Are you well, my lady?"

A maid, a sweet-faced thing and new to the castle, bustled in with a load of firewood and stumbled to the hearth. The countess's eyes lingered on her, sparkling with heat. "He still hasn't greeted me. Not one gift. They say he lost, that the Ottomans will swallow Sárvár soon."

The maidservant turned to leave.

"Stop, beautiful child," she murmured. "What is your name?"

"Talia, my lady," the girl said, keeping her eyes lowered.

Reka needed time. She needed Anna to live. The countess needed blood.

"I am hungry," the noblewoman said, parting her lips as if begging for water, keeping her eyes on the maid. "Come here Reka."

Fear coursed through Reka but she obeyed. Drawing close, the countess pulled her until Reka could feel the woman's hot breath in her ear. She tensed. But the countess only whispered.

When Reka rose, she stared down. She'd do as her lady bid, do everything as she had been directed, every detail, just as she had always done during her service here in the castle. Nausea moved through her, making her stomach tighten.

Reka beckoned the girl over, ordering her to lie next to the countess.

There, she lashed the girl, tight enough so she couldn't leave, then tighter so she couldn't move. By the time the girl realized this strange request was something dreadful, it was too late. Reka couldn't look at her. The girl pleaded for release, but Reka hurried to the door, looking back only once. The countess bared her teeth. The door shut and the screams began.

Reka ran down the hall as fast and far as she could go.

43

Like cake, constructed into delicate layers, decorated and crowned with fresh fruit. Admiration devolves into violent slicing, cake divided and finally consumed. It was the whole purpose of cake.

"Are you married, sir?"

The inquisitor has calmed down, he's telling himself not to be afraid, or angry, not to feel anything at all. "Yes," he says, curtly.

"Children? Daughters? I know someone who'd love to meet your daughters."

His face darkens.

The air laughs at him.

There is always someone, somewhere, eating cake.

—

The snow would not cease, falling for two days of tense waiting. Anna walked the corridors like a lost child, living only on coiled need for action.

Villagers who had come with the count numbered about thirty men, women, and children. They had been put to work quickly, filling in the desperately needed cracks in the serving staff. They lifted Anna's spirits, their voices bursting with mirth. The group brought a sense of home and normality that warmed Anna and gave her a reprieve as she waited for the snow to stop.

Despite the countess's dislike of the practice, newcomers slept in the hall out of necessity. After talking to a few of the younger ones, it seems that the count knew his wife well, or at least knew that she struggled to staff the castle in his absence. These were villagers who were displaced from the fighting on the southern border, they had been promised work at Sárvár. A chill prickled Anna's spine despite her spot near the hearth, many of the new servants talked in low tones with one another. The castle made everyone quieter, as if the towers pushed down on them.

"Wretched heathens," one of the men, called Gabor, complained.

A woman elbowed him in the ribs. "Are they really heathens? Have you ever considered that they have the same god as us?"

"How do you figure on that? They aren't part of the same church."

Marina rolled her eyes. "We aren't part of the same churches either. Look, Fabia over there, she still loves the Pope. Him by the fire, he's a Calvinist. And what are you? Loyal servant of God and all that is holy? Believer in the sanctity of marriage?" She began to laugh. Anna smiled in spite of herself. She took note and gave Anna a knowing look, one that said that they get it, even if the rest don't.

"Think the rumors are true?" Raakel asked. "About the bastard?"

"That may be, may be." Marina yawned and stretched. "I say, more power to the countess. Noblemen have enough bastards living out in towns, about time noble ladies did the same."

The fire flickered with a draft and the group grew quiet for a moment. Anna studied the flames, afraid to ask the wealth of questions that swirled within her.

"I heard there were two of them. The countess's girl and another child from her favorite servant."

Marina shushed the woman. "Enough gossip. We all know plenty of bastards and they're children like any else."

Anna's body energized. Two bastards. This had to be about Anna and her sister. Some servant. Who?

"What else you women gonna talk about if you don't gossip?" Gabor said, peering from under a cap, his voice cracking as he spoke. "That's what womenfolk do anyhow. Talk, talk, talk."

"Oh shush yourself too. God knows you're a bastard, you have bastards, and you act like a child."

To this the man grunted.

The women laughed, forgetting about Anna in the corner. A child whined to their mother and several people laid down into their bedrolls. Perhaps Anna should do the same.

Marina rocked thoughtfully. "Talia's been gone since this morning. Really, the girl, she keeps me worrying about her all the time. Wonder where she's made off to now."

"Off with the countess, didn't you know? I thought someone would've told you," Gabor said.

Marina laughed. "Well now, there's a good job for her."

Anna went cold. Words of warning came back to her, from Ficzkó and Reka— you aren't safe here. No one is safe here. We all know the pretty ones disappear.

Anna rose quietly and slipped out of the hall. She chided herself, hands shaking, as she entered the countess's residence. This was a rash plan—no, she had no plan at all—just a grasp at hope. Everything seemed to lead back to the countess and her instincts told her there may be clues here. If her mother served the countess personally, then perhaps she still did.

The empty bedchamber unfurled, walls of dark hardwood, carved with trees and snaking vines, so intricate and busy that it seemed as if the foliage lived. A breeze blew through the branches, letting a series of carved leaves free from their nests, perpetually dangling in a moment of movement. Lengths of scarlet fabric hung suspended from the ceiling, draping elegantly over a grand bed. Other shades of red upholstered two chairs and the overlapping carpets. An odd sweet smell curled her nose, mixed with the heavy scent of recently burned incense, and the cutting air of early winter pouring through the open window. A chamber overwhelmed by lusciousness but also a cold darkness.

She trod over the carpets, at first soft and pliable under her feet, but as she moved further into the chamber, the carpets changed, stiffened and, within another step, her slipper saturated with something wet. Scarlet liquid pooled over the scarlet floor. Coverlets on the bed rumpled and stained. The outline of handprints, barely visible, printed on the dark wood walls. Anna covered her mouth.

Unable to move, she took in the scene, amazed at the falseness of the room. What appeared lush a moment ago now weighed heavy and horror filled. A place of death.

Footsteps sounded in the hall.

Anna looked about wildly. No way of escaping. They'd find her.

Desperate, she threw herself onto the floor, feeling the stickiness under her fingers and cheek as she shimmied underneath the huge bed. She held back a gag at the sweet, copper scent. The edge of the crimson pool reached for her as if searching for its owner.

"Another cleanup." Ilona's husky forceful voice announced. "Our lady has been busy again it seems."

Someone choked in response.

"Oh come on now, woman," Ilona said. "How many times will this drive you to fall into pieces? You made your choices."

Their feet came into view and one of them dropped a wad of old linen over the carpet. Reka dropped to her knees, putting pressure on the carpet as she went, sopping up the sticky crimson. "Why do we allow this?" Reka's voice quivered.

"Allow?" Ilona laughed. "Who said anything about allow? What're we gonna do? Huh? Tell her not to? Better just to go on working, making the little bit to live and sometimes give some relief to these poor souls, when we can. Whether or not we resist, she will find her prey. There's nothing about us that can't be easily replaced."

Nobles are like fickle gods. Anna's father did not know the full horrible truth of his words.

Ilona moved about the room, the soft sound of cloth rubbed against the wood walls. Blood leaked through the linens, turning Reka's hands a haze of dark pink. The woman held them up and examined them, her lips stiff and eyes watery. "I'm sorry," she whispered.

"Come on now, hurry up, we'll put the linens in the fire after. Let's get this grim work done."

"Where's the body?"

Ilona paused, her hands dangling at her sides. "Never seen where some of them go, but others, that witch takes."

Witch. The old ugly thing that roamed the castle halls. They said she made the medicine that kept the countess's pain at bay.

Reka blotted closer to the bed, her pale hands near enough that

Anna could have reached out and held them. "We could tell someone. Get help."

"You gonna risk your boy over it?"

"No," Reka responded.

"Didn't think so."

They paused. "I hear them already. Scoot now, girl."

The door cracked and both Reka and Ilona's voices dipped low in a courteous greeting.

"You will practice discretion, wife, or for all that is holy, I will teach you discretion." The count's voice boomed. "A noble," he said, his voice rising in volume. "A goddamned noble girl. What you do with commoners, I care not. But a child of the nobility is not your right."

Erszébet's voice rose sharply, angry. "Don't you think I hear about what you do while traveling about Hungary playing at being a hero? You took her to bed."

A crack made Anna flinch and she dug her nails into her palms so she wouldn't cry out.

A barely audible intake of pain. The countess entered the chamber, weeping, her skirts pulling at the blood on the carpet.

Ferenc's voice thundered louder as he followed. "What right you had to concern yourself with such matters ended the moment you gave yourself to a commoner and bore his bastard child before we even wed."

Chilling silence. Anna held her breath.

"And this mess," he said.

"You don't know what it's like to wait endlessly and rot in some semblance of maternal dignity. This is my prison as much as it could be yours and I don't have the luxury of killing in the name of war. So I do what I can with what I have. How surprising, inmates may turn out to be exactly like their keepers."

Ferenc laughed, dark and heartless. "You've drawn the attention of the palatine. For now, Thurzó's much too busy with other matters involving the emperor and hasn't chosen to investigate because of our friendship. But you best work quietly before our estates appear an easy source to finance the emperor's plans. They'll descend on us, Erszébet. I'll survive it, but you, they won't be so merciful."

"You need me too much for an heir," the countess said. "Once you have your boy, then perhaps I will be afraid."

The blood had dried into crusted red flakes on Anna's face and in her hair, dying her dress and apron brown-black. Hours passed before she could bring herself to risk sneaking back out. She fled to the familiar washing rooms. Throwing herself into the filmy gray water of a bath long since used. It didn't matter, he scrubbed herself raw. She scrubbed as if she could wash away the foreboding that enveloped her soul.

44

He's not satisfied, the inquisitor, he holds his quill up like a blade.

"Where have they been buried?"

He's not listening again, the truth was laid over and over in front of him. It is vexing.

"Where the white flowers grow like a blanket of snow."

His face has flushed scarlet.

A crow calls outside.

—

The witch gave her beauties time and energy. After finding a girl, the witch worked tirelessly on her. That is when the beauty needed the witch most, to transform. Draining and replacing the blood took time, a process of injecting a liquid made of wine and lavender. Purify. Push through the rest of the blood and push out the foulness of the body. Stuffed them full of clay and submerged them in honey, the amber liquid infusing the flesh. They were unworked silver and the witch was the smithy, the fine hammer.

Not like men. The witch didn't ruin her beauties, force them to unravel and rot into motherhood and age. Instead, the witch coaxed them and comforted, ensured they rested and glittered forever. Perfect and beautiful always.

She could see the breath in front of her face as she worked. The table littered with an array of pretty things, pieces of lace, bits of ribbon, odd pieces from the count's wartime booty, jewelry and gems. A length of rope dangled from the cabin rafters.

This beauty, once a farmer girl, now lay upon the workbench, ready to transform into untouchable perfection.

The needle pricked the witch's thumb and she winced, sucking on the wound and studying her work.

Even after, the girl's eyes still judged.

Disgust.

Downturned lips.

Scorn.

The witch sewed a sweet pout, a pleasing stain of crimson.

Perfect. Fairest.

The other girls always whispered, crowding around the witch, peering over her work. Jealous.

Her lips sulked. Stitches must be loose, sloppy. The witch rethreaded the needle.

Eyes that were orbs that sang and whispered. *You'll never be me.*

"But I was, wasn't I? Didn't I take you just like you asked me? Perfect, you said."

A faint tinkle of laughter fell like music from somewhere above, the cold bit into the witch's sallow cheeks.

You are disgusting. Look at you, ugly old thing, shriveled up before you even wrinkled up.

Tears stung her eyes, shutting them tight as if the force of her lids could keep out the words. "Stop it!"

Rolls of old fat, skin lumped and pockmarked. You'll never be me.

"STOP IT!"

The girl's voice had gotten so loud, so loud. The witch couldn't think. "Stop it. Stop it. Stop it."

She reached for the tiny shards of mirrors on a workbench, her cold fingers barely able to feel for them. *Cow. Cunt. Dirt. Your mother's still here, looking for you.* The witch shrieked, pushing down the coin sized shards onto her eyes, a shiny reflection . . . her shiny reflection. Relief flooded her chest. Shut her up. Except for her whispers, the longing sighs and soft giggles, the brush of soft curls against our skin. The way her girls should be.

Make me perfect.

"I am, my darling."

The witch cut the thread.

45

The snow had slowed until the sparse flakes floated rather than fell from the sky. Anna spotted Pál across the courtyard. Navigating through servants, she greeted some familiar faces, all of them new to the castle. Several of the men hauled fresh timber and made to patch the damage from the storm. Everything moved a little slower as they worked through the heavy snowfall on the ground.

Anna whispered to Pál. "Where's your mother?"

The boy gave her a blank look and shrugged before darting away. Aggravated, Anna almost ran after him, but too many people would see. The buzz of voices came from everywhere all at once and no sign of Reka. Where did the woman go? Surely the woman noted that the snow had ceased.

A hand closed around Anna's arm, dragging her into a darkened corridor. Strong hands pushed her roughly against the doorframe, trapping her there. She looked into the count's eyes. For half a moment, she almost didn't recognize him this close.

"There you are. I've been searching for you." He smiled pleasantly as if he'd just met her for a friendly chat.

"My lord," Anna breathed. Fear stabbed her intestines. Did he know she had hidden in the countess's chamber?

"Since the moment I spotted you, I have been able to think of little else." The count pressed himself against her, tangling his fingers in her hair. His face so close that the whiskers of his beard scraped along her jaw.

She froze, her breath escaping in ragged pulses.

"Do you know what I want?" he asked.

What he wanted was abundantly clear and the way he handled her, looked at her, it all spoke of ownership, nauseating entitlement to her and her body. Another thought chilled Anna. What would happen if he pressed her further? Undressed her? What would happen if he saw what he could not understand? She tried to wiggle free but Ferenc held her fast, running a hand along her waist.

"I would have thought you'd have more discretion, husband."

So terrified, Anna hadn't heard the footfalls of the countess standing mere steps away. With a curse, the count released her. Anna stumbled against the wall before awkwardly regaining her balance.

"She is pretty." The countess gazed at Anna coolly. "But I suppose they all are."

"More beautiful than you. Once, you were indeed the fairest, but now you're nothing but a Báthory bitch," he said.

The countess's face turned to stone. "Run along, little servant girl."

Anna needed no further urging. She sprinted away, back into the harried courtyard. Tears of shame and fear stung her eyes.

"Has anyone seen Talia?" A woman's voice called out with a tenor of suppressed worry. "Has anyone seen my daughter?"

Anna wiped her nose, moving through and toward the washroom. She hoped to hide before calling any further attention to herself. A shadow fell in step next to her.

"We best hurry then," Reka said. The maidservant regarded Anna seriously. "Come on, it is time. Your sister is waiting."

—

They reached the sloping floor that led to the castle basement. Reka lit a candle. The flame exaggerated the scars on her face, turning the woman into a crone with each flicker. Anna had to work to quiet her mind, to ignore the prickles on her skin and clench of her jaw. Reka motioned Anna forward, her expression tight. The darkness before them grew like a creeping weed into the unknown depths of the tunnel. Stopping before an odd low hatch, Reka grasped the pull ring. "We have to crawl," she said.

"Alright," Anna whispered, and followed close behind.

Inside, the scent of urine, more concentrated then anything found in the washroom where she often used urine to boil away stains. Pál had been waiting for them, holding a tiny lantern, his still baby-like face grim. Tattered cloth piled on the floor. Otherwise, empty. Reka gasped.

"She was gone when I got here," Pál said helplessly. "No sign of her."

Reka shook her head and gave Anna a guilty look. "She had been ill-treated . . . I didn't think she had the strength to go anywhere without help."

So close. Anna pulled at the tattered pile of cloth, her eyes misted with frustration. Something had been scratched on the floor beneath them. She pushed the rest of the cloth away. "What is it?" Reka asked, crouching closer. Into the packed dirt, words carved with a shaky hand. *Meet me, dear sister, on the other side.*

"Nusi," Anna sighed, "almost found you."

Reka mouthed the words thoughtfully. "Perhaps she's gone ahead?"

"Gone ahead to where?"

"Ilona once told me that the castle basement leads to a tunnel. A passage carved into the earth. Maybe your sister knows of it." Reka titled her head. "It is the best chance for you and Pál to escape."

The grief of loss threatened to overwhelm as Anna traced her fingers over the words.

Reka put a gentle hand on Anna's back, patting her, trying to reassure her. "You need to go now. If the count has marked you for his, so has the countess. It won't be long before one or the other will descend upon you."

—

Pál followed behind, his mother ahead, his step echoed regret in the darkness. Urgency washed over Anna and she could barely keep herself from leading. She had to believe Nusi waited for her on the other side of this tunnel. They would leave and not come back. She'd tell the magistrate and the clergy in town, tell them of the things she had seen. Remorse washed over Anna. She would never know her mother. Never find answers. She'd need to make her peace with that.

Reka stopped. "I won't go further," she said. "My absence will be noted." Her sad eyes fell on Pál. "Take good care of him."

The boy reached for his mother. Reka caught his hand in her own, giving it a tight squeeze and kissed it.

"I will," Anna whispered.

Mother and son released each other. Reka took a candle from her apron. She lit it on the lantern flame before passing it to Anna. Pál did not look up.

"Thank you," Anna said, suddenly sad for the boy.

"No," Reka responded, "thank you for helping my son."

As the pair watched, darkness swallowed Reka's light and Anna put a hand on Pál's shoulder. "Come on." The boy nodded and they turned to trudge into their own darkness, holding aloft the flame, imagining what terrors may lay in wait for them in the velvet blackness. A panicked shout sounded behind them, making them twirl toward where Reka had stood not more than a moment before.

"Mom!" Pál took off.

"Wait," Anna yelled, trying to grab for him and missing. She ran behind him, hoping desperately she'd catch him before whatever or whoever had surely caught Reka. All Anna could hear were her own pounding feet, the rush of darkness flooding her hair. The muscles in her legs burned, making her stumble on the uneven floor. She didn't see him, hadn't realized he was there until he plucked her up and crushed her to his chest with his single arm.

"Shhhh," Ficzkó said. "Calm down, Anna. It's okay, it's okay."

She thrashed against him. She didn't know where Pál had gone.

The smell of sweat rose off of Ficzkó. "Please," he said. "I must follow the countess's commands. Please don't make this worse. I told you to run. Why didn't you listen?"

Anna searched wildly. Reka lay at his feet, her eyes closed, her chest rising and falling in rapid little shudders. Anna's mind, a swollen mass of confusion, thoughts mumbling in a series of rapid and then impossibly slow realizations. Ficzkó held her tighter. Anna stared at Reka and struggled to breathe in his crushing grip.

"She fell," he explained. "She'll be okay. You'll be okay."

A trembling took over Anna's body. She managed to whisper. "No one here is okay."

46

Coming back to Sárvár always made Ferenc angry. The walls had a way of blocking out the green and blue, of shrinking the world and sapping vitality. Reality existed here in the form of ceaseless responsibility. Letters to write, dictate and sign. Squabbles between the peasants, household provisions and repair. Even begetting heirs felt like responsibility. But so far Erszébet had only given him girls.

He had bastards, some he knew about and others he didn't care to. But only one lived here in the castle of Sárvár. One, if needed, could be legitimized and declared the fruit of the Báthory-Nádasdy pairing. He supposed it couldn't hurt to sprinkle more bastards within the castle. One of the new servants slept in his bed, curled like a content cat. Ferenc pinched her.

"Get up," he said.

The girl blinked in confusion, her pupils dilating and retracting as she roused from the warmth of sleep and fancy coverlets.

Sounds of shuffling outside the door fouled Ferenc's mood before the inevitable knock followed. Damn it, he'd been avoiding it all for too long. They'd be wanting his decision on this or that. The girl scrabbled up, gathering and clutching her clothing to her chest.

The door opened and Erszébet strode in looking like a starched red fan. Her aging had never been more apparent. The servant mumbled apologies, ducking her head, and ran from the room only partially clothed. Ferenc laughed.

Erszébet did not.

—

On the other side.

Too many memories, some of them Anna recognized, others faded in and out through a haze of drowsy nausea. Part of her refused to surface and huddled to the deep root of sleep. But her body demanded awareness and urgent action. She tried to bolt up and a rough circle of rope tightened against her neck, forcing her to remain prone and unable to see the entire room. Already the coarse fiber of the rope left her neck raw. Straw itched through her clothing. Hands and feet were bound together like a pig ready for roasting.

Should have never come here. No one comes back.

Muscles begged for movement, she managed to bend her knees to relieve some of the discomfort.

"Hello?" Anna called.

No one answered.

"Reka? Is that you?" Anna whispered, hopeful.

Her eyes burned and welled and words clung to her soul, pushing a dark fear into her that promised to turn red. "I'm so sorry. So sorry." Words meant for her sister and, finally, for herself. They never come back.

A shuffle outside the room and the door swung open. Ilona stared down, her face pinched, knife in hand. Anna swallowed a scream.

Ilona's hands were on Anna, sticky, cutting at her bonds. "Keep quiet," Ilona said, her face shifted and twitched nervously. "Follow me." With a jerky motion, the older woman held open the door wide, licking her lips, and said, "Hurry."

Eagerly, blood drumming in her ears, Anna pushed herself from the bed. She could only think how she longed for the wind and to be free of the castle's brick and stone walls.

"Hurry," Ilona said.

The pair moved quickly through the empty courtyard.

—

Brisk morning cold had wormed its way into the wires of his beard as he pushed his horse harder, whipping over the gentle sloping hills. Ferenc imagined how he would position troops here and where the Ottomans, or even the Habsburgs, would come at him. He saw carnage on the ground and how all were defeated before him. His thoughts left him exhilarated and disappointed when he returned to the stables.

No stable boy came to meet him. Instead, his calls were met with a restless quiet. Echoing his irritation, his steed let out a phlegmy snort. No matter, he was quite capable of stabling his own horse. He swung himself down and guided the steed inside. The horses shifted, one stomped and paced in her stall. Ferenc worried for her, the absence of a stable hand had made her nervous. He would have the hands punished. Perhaps the horses hadn't even had their feed.

"It's alright, girl." Ferenc patted the horse gently. The stall door let out a scraping sound as he pushed it open. "It's alright, girl." The horse stepped from her stall eagerly, hooves leaving red half-moons. Within, the straw streaked in crimson.

He recognized the servant girl he had spent the night with, she curled protectively over herself. Deep claw-like wounds rent through the girl's body and face. Where her flesh had not been broken, it mapped a crisscross of new bruises and swelling. Little left to admire about her now. Those wound patterns resembled ones he had committed on the flesh of many Ottomans. The clawed glove he had eventually gifted to Erszébet, a new toy to keep the Báthory bloodlust busy.

Ferenc cursed and slammed the stall shut, making the mare start and bolt.

Erszébet.

He clenched his fist.

Báthory witch.

He had thought the same thing after he watched her smirk at the body of her lover hanging over the wall so many years ago. If only he could be rid of her and still maintain the lands and wealth she brought to the union. He retrieved the mare, muttering kindnesses and led her to an empty stall.

Perhaps he could.

When he returned to his quarters, Ferenc had the stable master summoned. As he waited for the man to arrive, Ferenc pulled out parchment and scribbled an idea to his friend, Lord Thurzó. For once, the scratch of the quill in his hands satisfied him almost as much as the sword.

47

Ilona pulled at Anna's sleeve across the darkening courtyard. "You were right to go beneath the castle. This time keep going. I'll find Pál."

"Where's Reka?" Anna said, breathlessly.

"I don't know," Ilona said, a shadow passing over her face. "Go."

Anna found herself moving carefully through the shadows, flitting from corner to corner. In her mind, the countess watched and knew Anna's every move. When she finally reached the entrance to the basement, she ran wildly, half-stumbling on the sloping floor. She passed the empty spot where Reka had lain.

The floor leveled, changing from brick to fitted stones, and then this soon gave way to dirt. A putrid smell invaded the darkness and soon its sticky sweetness clung to her clothing, seeping into her pores. Up ahead, something moved. Anna stopped, holding the candle high to get a good look. Her hands shook. The source of the smell.

Bodies, piles of them, thrown haphazardly into what had clearly become a trash heap of human flesh. Bare bones jutted from the lower layers, putrefied green and black molds crusting over others, gaping mouths, eyeless faces, hair barely clinging to rotted scalps. Over top, the freshest bodies sprawled, their eyes still set in their faces like shocked dolls, arms thrown open as if seeking a last embrace. All girls.

"Don't look," she told herself, but she couldn't tear her gaze away.

A wave of darkness moved over the heaps, enveloping, scurrying over fresh and rotted flesh alike. The girls disappeared behind a curtain, forgotten forever. Everything that they were in life submerged under the indiscriminate gnawing of rats.

The countess destroyed more than beauty. She spoiled it. She took hope. Keeping dreams in check. She'd do it, again and again.

And again.

Could her sister be there too, piled beneath?

Nusi waited for her on the other side. Anna had to believe that. Holding a sleeve over her face, Anna rushed past and deeper into the tunnel, leaving behind the sound of a hundred feasting rats.

—

To György Thurzó, Palatine of Hungary

I wish to summon you and your attendants to my estate in Sárvár with urgency. By God's grace I have arrived, but there has been no rest for me. Instead, I have discovered what a husband wishes never to discover, that his wife has committed unspeakable acts against God. I have discovered the Countess Báthory a murderer of servant and noble girls alike. With a heavy heart, I implore you to arrive so that I may show you proof.

Ferenc Nádasdy

48

Ficzkó trailed the girl. He had intended to talk to her before Erszébet summoned her for whatever sick games she played. What if he had saved Anna from that fate? What if, instead of even letting the countess have her, he whisked Anna away to safety? The witch's face flashed in his mind, the growth of her belly matching Erszébet's. Who had fathered the witch's child? He knew the answer already, didn't he?

The cries of those babies as they were smuggled into the night still rang in his ears, as did the sound of the man's insides slipping from his body and smacking against the whitewash wall as he hung.

His missing hand tingled with heat, as if suddenly buried in a newly slaughtered calf. Down deeper he went, under the castle, until the air dampened and grew stagnant. The sickly sweet scent of rot clouded about him. Then, he found the pile of girls. Ficzkó recognized pieces of them, scraps of their clothing. It all became real and horrible.

Sinking to his knees, everything he'd been, exposed. He'd sold his humanity for any sliver of power over another. All these putrefying girls, he'd ruined them long before Erszébet did. His thoughts turned to Susanna. His hand came across something hard on the floor, smooth and light in his palm. He lifted it up to the light.

A small wooden cross. The one he'd seen Susanna with long ago. He raised the flame, scattering rats. There, he drew closer, instantly recognizing the tattered dress. A skeleton, long stripped of flesh, gaped the truth back at him. Bones gnawed by generations of rats. This is where she'd gone.

He had been angry at her for so long, for leaving him behind. Throwing him away. He could still feel the cold, earthen floor of their cottage when they were still children, trying to scrape together the food. His fist tightened over the cross.

She'd never gone anywhere at all. Forever trapped beneath the castle. Just like all the girls he sent down there. Ficzkó bowed his head and forced himself to breathe in the rot.

———

Anna emerged in the woods, trees standing spindly black against the night. Her protesting body, draining quickly of adrenaline, left her lightheaded and confused. No sign of Nusi. Only fear and the need to escape pushed her forward through the dark. If she stopped, she'd freeze, so better to keep moving, even if that meant becoming exhausted and lost.

Tiny lights twinkled ahead, glimpses of hope between the trees. Desire surged forth. Perhaps her sister waited there. She quickened her pace.

Light, fluffy snow flaked through the canopy, floating like dancing fairies coming to rest on leaves and branches in muffled chimes, music to guide her forward.

A cabin soon emerged, partially enveloped by nature. Roots had invaded the foundation, shadows of vegetation climbing over walls, naked vines swirling through the windows and running like confused, tiny rivers over rotten versions of itself from seasons past. The cabin seemed a good place to take shelter for the night, for her sister to have lighted candles as a signal to Anna. With relief, she knocked on the rickety door.

The woods whispered and rustled as she waited. Snowflakes brushed her cheeks. Anna knocked again. On squealing hinges, the door cracked open as if giving entrance, beckoning inside.

"Hello?" Anna said, taking an uneasy step.

From a corner, a familiar face rocked in a chair by the candlelight. The witch from the castle, her eyes shone like oily wash water. The door slammed shut behind Anna and she let out a yelp of surprise.

"Come in, come in," the witch said. "You seem frightfully cold."

Anna didn't move. "I'm sorry," she said. "I needed shelter. I was looking for my sister."

"Yes, of course." The witch continued to rock. "She is here and here is warm."

A small fire licked in the hearth, giving out blessed heat. Anna's flesh yearned for it. The idea of going back into the cold night made her spirit shrivel. Glancing about the room, slow appreciation overtook her. A magical world sprawled within the cabin.

Tables filled with beautiful things, bits of lace and silks, embroidered patches, dried flowers and fine chains of gold and silver. Another table with an assortment of jewels, some free from fetters, others nestled in equally precious metals. Anna's breath caught.

The witch watched her with glittering eyes, still rocking. "Sister sleeps."

Anna sank stiffly into a half-broken chair.

"Must be hungry, so hungry." The witch stood, moving jerkily toward a corner stockpiled with foodstuff.

"Yes, a bit," Anna answered.

Rummaging, the witch found what she searched for, plucking it out and holding it aloft in victory. "Very good food here. Delicious."

An apple. A perfect beauty of a fruit, something like what Eve must have plucked from the Garden of Eden. The witch shoved it forward, offering the apple to Anna. It rested in the witch's extended knobby hand, a perfect sphere of crimson so dark and ripened that it appeared almost black.

Anna's mouth watered at the sight. Nusi faded from her mind. She knew only that she wanted this apple more than anything she's ever wanted. To tear its flesh and grind its core and make it part of herself.

The witch smiled and urged again.

Anna accepted, feeling the apple's pleasant weight, the skin smooth to the touch. She brought the fruit to her lips and sunk her teeth into the soft flesh. Juices poured over her senses like honey.

"Good," the witch said.

Anna closed her eyes, feeling the flesh of the apple in her mouth, waves of floral flavor. She could smell the blossom from which the fruit was born. A supernatural sense of being pulsed through her consciousness, as if her legs were the roots of the tree and this apple was one she had borne like a mother. Anna ate her child. The idea didn't horrify her. In fact, she could only take bite after bite, unable to stop the appalling act.

"This is where I keep my favorite things," the witch said. She watched Anna chew and swallow. Her gaze moved from the apple to the mouth that fed upon it. "I have more to show you. Sister is here."

The witch opened another door, one Anna hadn't noticed. A shimmering light poured in from beyond it. "Come."

As Anna passed through the doorway, more wonders sprawled before her, a clearing within the forest, hewn from walls of thicket and vine. Light reflected and refracted from hundreds of candles and mirrors, summoning images of themselves over and over again. The mirrors lined the living walls, forming a large hall that only seemed possible in imaginations and stories of fairy courts. Shards of glass glittered a pathway through the center. Anna moved forward, dreamlike, in dry-eyed fascination, toward a series of glass encasements. The apple fell from her hand.

Coffins made of glass. Within each laid a dead girl. Beautiful, pale-fleshed maids, so pale they looked molded from the snow that pillowed them. Bits of ribbon and flowers woven through their hair, breasts with lace sewn into unresponsive flesh, jewels choked from mouths. Pearls dropped like tears from their eyes. Others didn't have eyes at all, but mirrors.

Anna whirled, looking franticly at each girl.

"See, my favorite things," the witch proclaimed, holding out an arm in pride.

Anna shrieked.

All those tiny mirrored eyes, impassive and cold, only reflected Anna's hapless terror. She gasped for air, her feet would not obey. Coffin after coffin loomed in her vision, flames and mirrors spinning. Anna began to fall, a descent that seemed to last forever, stuck in a moment of terrible knowing. She'd die here, just all these girls had. When she finally hit the ground, she could only shiver in fear, her treacherous limbs motionless despite her mind's command to run.

"I've waited for you for so long. So very long, Snow White." the witch said. "I will make you perfect."

The witch came into view. An odd smile wrinkled her features, as she pulled a mask over her face.

Anna couldn't scream anymore, couldn't weep, but her soul exploded into dismay and raw grief. The witch wore a mask made from flesh, raven hair still affixed above the high forehead, and Anna knew. Her sister was worse than dead.

"Perfect, perfect, Snow White," the witch said, words passing through the dead sister's mouth.

49

Ficzkó stumbled out of the tunnel into the thick of the woods, sucking in clean cold air, trying to get the scent of death out of his lungs, a heavy boulder of guilt in his heart. Susanna's quiet features looked back from within his mind. If only she would have stayed close, he could have kept her safe. But he'd lost them all. Susanna and Elek. And now, not one, but perhaps two children he sired.

Each of the girls' he'd abused before giving them over to Erszébet flipped through is mind, their burning eyes full with fear and rage. He had abused them, tricked them, and took from them. They pressed on him now, their harsh whispers of condemnation stuffing his mind. He didn't deserve any of their mercy.

Lights up ahead, dancing in the night woods like spirits, beckoned him.

—

Snow White's eyes shifted wildly while the witch stroked the girl's hair. "I found you," the witch hummed. She had secrets to tell, things to teach. Searching for so long and to have the fairest one finally here and ready to become. Warmth spread throughout the witch's body, the closest she'd ever felt to joy. So many

211

secrets. She leaned forward, touching her lips to Snow White's ear. "Remember this, fair one. There are no princes. No knights. These are just ideas they tell girls, to keep them believing. And we do. We believe until we learn how to hunt for ourselves. Then we hunt each other." With a long sigh, the witch straightened.

In the center of the hall of mirrors, she had long ago erected the glass bed for the fairest one. She'd gathered branches and sticks for months to form the base to raise it above all the others. The bed atop glittered in the myriad of encircling candles. Collecting snow in a cloth she began the process of packing it within the glass. To be kept forever.

The witch had already chosen the ornaments as well, crystals, pearls, white lace, and silver chains. Yet her favorite choice by far were the corpse poppies woven into a crown of petaled white and delicate inner reds.

All for her Snow White. The fairest one.

The witch touched her beauty with careful fingers, gentle as caresses as she laid Snow White within her bed. The sight overwhelmed the witch, this girl she had dreamed about for so long. This one, who had called to her and asked over and over for a name.

Snow White. The witch wanted to shout it to the heavens. All these years. The other girls called from their glass cases.

I'm the perfect one.

The most beautiful.

You loved me most.

The witch smiled and nodded to herself as they bickered. "You were until she arrived. But I still cherish you all. Still love you. But it's her that I crown." The old man shifted underground, laughing to himself. Watching and cooing over the scene. "She will be mine. All of her," the witch whispered. She stripped away Snow White's apron, pulled at the blouse. The girl's eyes widened, longing to speak, to move. Murmuring comforts, the witch continued with her work. Each layer of cloth, a regrettable cover over art she'd find beneath. She waited for the awe. It always came when she undressed her beauties, disrobing them so that the witch could know all of them, the depth of them and take, for herself, the gowns of their glamor. And finally, transform the beauties into the perfection they would forever obtain. No threat of aging, no one to ruin them with hardship and sorrow. The witch loved them always, appreciated them.

She inhaled. The last remnant of cloth remained and the witch pulled, letting it fall away. The awe came, but in a way she'd never expected. Trembling and aghast, then melding into adoration, the witch knew the truth. This girl had been born with the parts allocated to men.

The witch stumbled, her mind whirling in confusion. The body before her glittered with more truth and more beauty than she could have ever imagined. Exquisitely lovely.

Reaching for her Snow White, the witch touched her face in wonder.

—

Ficzkó threw open the door, still clutching Susanna's cross, which formed a solid center of his rage. He needed the truth, damn it, all of it. Lurching through the doorway, he rushed into a scene that caused him to falter. An outdoor hall, lavished with candles and shattered glass, ran the length of wall-like growth. For long moments, he could only gawk at what unfurled before him. White poppies grew softer than the deepest snowfall, crowding around mirrors and crystalline cases. He looked closer, his heart seizing with grief and horror. Girls rested within each glass case—no, these were coffins.

Tombs for the beautiful dead, each decorated with riches and elegance. Some wore satin and silks, others nothing at all, jewels spilling from their gaping mouths. Ficzkó recognized too many of them. Worst of all, he still wanted them.

This girl, plucked from a farm. That girl, sold to Ficzkó by her father. Nameless and forgotten. And in the middle of it all stood the witch.

"Dory," he roared.

He had been so wrong to feel sorrow for her, to wonder at the abuses she experienced. He allowed himself to remember the night she'd come upon him and Erszébet, the night he'd reenacted upon other girls. Vague memories of poisoned apples and weakness, the truth had always been within him.

"What did you do to me? To Susanna? To them?"

The witch turned, pulling a mask from her face, a thing with dark hair still attached. Dark hair, so like Anna's. Ficzkó wanted to fall to his knees, wanted to strike at the witch for taking first what should have belonged to him. His. Too late. Her odd expression and gray flesh, even now, brought forth pity. He had once called her a friend.

"You've taken everything good I could have been," he said.

"Me?" the witch asked. "You became all on your own." She moved forward like a snake. "Do you like me? Am I not beautiful? I too became all on my own. I loved you once."

Tears stung his eyes. "Love doesn't take. It doesn't force your will upon others."

Laughter, the witch shook, struggling to catch her breath. "And you know the nature of love? You?"

From within a glass coffin, a faint movement, barely perceptible but he forced himself to believe. The girl within still lived, even if barely. "What have you done?"

The witch stopped. "What have *you* done, dear Ficzkó?"

"I gave you kindness. I advocated for you."

The witch's voice soured. "You gave me pity."

Ficzkó edged closer, finally getting a glimpse of the girl within the glass. Anna. The girl still lived.

"This girl," Ficzkó breathed hard, "is my daughter." He shuddered, could still feel the violation, the way his body responded and how he wanted so much for it to stop. He had shut the molestation out for so long, denying, unbelieving. "Erszébet birthed my child. You did too, didn't you? And you killed Susanna."

Something in the witch's eyes flickered. "I loved you."

Anna moaned. The sound echoed against the mirrors and his soul. Everything he'd done, nothing would make it better. No God or sister would ever forgive him.

"You should have loved me. Not your own sister. Not like that. Not Erszébet. And her too, Erszébet should have loved me like you loved her. But I had your child. Yes. We still became as one, you and I created a child."

"I would have never chosen to give you child. Never. You took that from me and you birthed this girl." Ficzkó pointed to Anna.

The witch chuckled low and merciless. "I had no daughter. The countess had your daughter. I gave birth to your boy . . . " Her words trailed and she looked toward the coffin, abrupt insight set her mouth in a straight line, eyebrows rising. "No," the witch mouthed. "We had a son."

A lithe sculpture of alabaster and unshed tears, Anna's nudity roused Ficzkó's desire. He gazed upon the girl, the exposed flesh, following the current to her secret parts. "She's our daughter." Ficzkó picked up a cloak and draped it over Anna.

"I did what they asked me," The witch said, swaying. "What they always ask me." She stumbled on the glass shards, causing them to crunch and chime softly.

The mirrors fragmented the witch's image into hundreds of pieces.

"She . . . she called to me. Snow White, so pure. She always calls and I answer." The witch gazed at the girl. "I don't understand. You are my Snow White."

Ficzkó bowed his head, sickened to his soul.

"There are no princes," the witch said, lifting her chin to look at him with a sneer. "And you couldn't be one if you tried."

Anna opened her eyes, pools of darkness, pupils expanding then contracting. Ficzkó's mind raced and he bowed his head, trying to hide his shame.

An odd, startled gasp erupted from the witch and her eyes widened. That gray-fleshed thing, face like a hilly landscape, sank until her cheek touched the shard-filled ground. A million lacerations formed, the witch welling blood onto the white poppies. Veins released themselves of the poison that resided within her soul.

Ilona stood behind the witch in triumph. "There's no need for princes when there're old girls still around." In her hand, a large glass shard dripped with the witch's blood. Reka rushed to Anna and gathered the girl into her arms.

Ficzkó had thought Reka wounded, but here she spit on the ground before him, and flashed hot rage as she draped Anna's arm over her shoulder. "You own nothing, little man. The count knows the truth. Even now his dogs are out to find you. To punish the commoner who fucked his countess."

The witch writhed on the ground, shouting angrily at voices only she could hear.

"I brought those babies out of the castle." Ilona glared at Ficzkó. "Me. None of you people deserved those little souls. Wasn't their fault, being born to you. I know who you are, both of you *and* that count and countess. I've known and watched and bided my time."

"I'm trying to save Anna," Ficzkó said. "Please let me atone for what I've done."

Ilona's boots crunched glass, weapon still in hand. She shoved a finger into his chest. "You're trying to save yourself. All those girls won't forgive you, even if they could. The moment you laid your eyes on them, they died."

Reka guided Anna carefully past the mirrors and hedges. The sun had just begun to pierce the canopy. Crisp air promised a new swell of snow.

———

"You're safe now, sweet Anna," Reka said.

The girl tried to speak. She mouthed indecipherable things. Whatever poison resided in her body would take time to flush way.

"Tell me again," Reka urged gently, leaning close, straining to listen. Lips fluttered against her cheek, but finally she heard. A rambling prayer-like litany, repeated.

"My name is Snow White."

50

Ferenc Nádasdy's letter had reached György Thurzó, Pálatine of Hungary. Not long after, the Pálatine came to Sárvár and found all the death that Erszébet had done and took her to some far off castle. Rumors were that the countess had been bricked into a room.

"Only 55?" Thurzó's official inquisitor was a plain man with a long mustache and a large mole on his left cheek.

The witch could only stare at that spot, chew her lip, and nod. Voices still called to her, like a symphony, crying for an artist. *Make us perfect.* She wanted them to burn too.

"How did you come into her ladyship's service?" the inquisitor asked.

It would be a painful end, but right. She would burn. And so would all the voices and her own horrid face.

"Picked me up from the road, on her way to Sárvár from Écsed."

The man peered up from his parchment, with something akin to stern disapproval. "On the road?"

"Yes."

He dipped his quill and scribbled. "Did you assist her in these offenses?"

"Yes." She could already see the flames, feel the searing heat.

"Why?" The question followed quickly, crisping on his lips.

217

"Because," she said, her fingers entwined as if her hands sought to choke one another. "She made me worth something."

The inquisitor's mustache twitched and he paused. Again, he dipped the quill and the scratching resumed. When he finished, he looked up and something passed over his face, a kind of pity and sadness. "May God have mercy on your soul."

The voices would be gloriously silent. But her own?

"They will execute you soon." The official moved uncomfortably. His shoulders hunched.

Perhaps there was never silence. Would this man hear her voice long after she was gone? Would he pass that along to another that would forever hear him? The idea unnerved her.

"600," she said, suddenly.

He looked up.

"There will always be girls." The witch leaned forward. "Always calling for perfection. Always dying."

—

Erszébet's hands shook as she signed her name and let the parchment curl unto itself. Part of her still wanted to rail against it, to make demands of her jailers, but she had been here long enough to know that no one cared. She pushed the document through the small window that served as her only gateway to the outside world. Nowadays, her thoughts were on how to avoid discomfort and when the next meal would be delivered. She made exchanges whenever possible for small things that made the time more bearable. If she signed this declaration, her jailers promised to bring someone to sing for her. Something sweet and innocent, albeit poor in quality, emanated from outside the brick. Small rewards for big sacrifices.

She had written her name and there would be nothing more.

I decree that the boy known as Pál Nádasdy is the son of my husband, Lord Nádasdy, and my own flesh. He is therefore entitled to all the honors befitting his position as son of the Nádasdy name.

Countess Erszébet Báthory

51

The year 1592
Scent of smoke curled around the witch's nose as if the preparation of some feast had begun. She gazed upon the crowd of people who had gathered from Sárvár, eager to watch and horrified all at once. She danced as the logs burned beneath her feet. She screamed and shrieked as the flames licked up and surrounded her. She knew nothing but agony.

Through the fire, girl faces stared. They'd die too, some at the hands of husbands and fathers. Others, the slow death of poverty or self-hatred would take them. Always the prey. No one would write down their names. They'd pass from memory like ghosts.

Her mother's voice cut through her dimming awareness.

Perfect. Most wonderful to look upon.

The witch sighed.

Under the ground they buried what was left of her and just like her mother, Dorottya Széntes wiggled and writhed until finally, she too, swam with the roots.

ONCE UPON A TIME...

. . . in the woods of Hungary, 1552.

The swell of Hanga Széntes's stomach had made walking difficult, but she still managed to find her way from Écsed. The baby would come soon, her body already longing to push the child out. She found a spot, pulling at the blankets she had packed and settled herself on them.

She'd do this alone. Make her way alone. Lady Báthory would've had Hanga killed before she even gave birth, ridding herself of them both. "You've bewitched my husband," the noblewoman had declared.

"Half the court's bewitched him, some not willingly," Hanga had replied.

A contraction stole her breath. She'd have this child. What came after that, she did not know.

FAIREST FLESH

AUTHOR'S NOTE

This is a fictional account of 16th Century Hungary and the world of Erszébet Báthory. But ultimately, this isn't only Erszébet's story, it is also about the people who surrounded her, participated and contributed to her crimes. Dorottya, Ficzkó, Ilona and Susanna were all involved in some way, although their type of involvement, personalities, ages and backgrounds depicted here are fictional. While there are several suggestions of the Countess's motivations such as stress, jealousy, and supernatural beliefs, the real reasons and number of the murders committed are no clearer now than during her trial. Reka, Mirella, Nusi and Agoston are purely fictional individuals, despite their vivid life inside my imagination. There was however, reports that a girl named Anna had been saved, perhaps the Countess's last victim and the only one we know of that managed to survive. Ilona (known as Ilona Jó), despite her depiction as a sort of heroine in the book was implicated in Erszébet's crimes and executed.

Further, I focused solely on the Nádasdy castle at Sárvár for ease of storytelling and the importance I wanted the castle to play in the story. However, the Nádasdy's maintained other properties such as the castle at Csejte in which many of Erszébet's crimes were committed.

Those aware of Báthory's history will note departures from the historical accounts. In order to make the timeline fit the ages and experiences of the characters, there are many deviations in this book from the actual timeline. The investigation, arrest and subsequent trail of Erszébet and her associates did not occur until the beginning of the 17th century. Ferenc for example died in

1604, several years before Erszébet (1614). He did however, gift his wife with the wicked claw-like glove that is believed to have been something he obtained during his military ventures. He also did take on the Báthory name as the prestige of the family outweighed the Nádasdy's. The Báthory family are titans of Hungarian history, a fact often obscured in the Western world by Erszébet's legacy. Members of the family at differing times served as Palatine of Hungary, Grand Duke of Lithuania, Voivode of Transylvania, Prince of Transylvania as well as King of Poland.

Báthory is often portrayed as bathing in the blood of young women, but this is a modern mythology. The true crimes committed by Báthory were so much worse. While unlikely that any sort of "blood baths" occurred, accounts of torture such as my depiction of the murder of the innkeeper's daughter abound. Victims of Báthory varied in age from approximately sixteen to as young as eleven. All were girls.

Those implicated in Erszébet's crimes faced harsh sentences. Dorottya, Ficzkó and Ilona Jó were tortured, killed and their bodies burned. Erszébet, being a noble woman of high standing and significant connections was bricked up in her castle at Csejthe where she eventually died in 1614.

It was a significant challenge, to locate in English, historical resources on several facets of this story, a shortcoming of my own Hungarian language disability. Because of this, when researching daily life within a 17th century Hungarian castle, I was forced to shelve my inner historian in service to the story. There is only so much time an author should spend on researching 16th century door latches before losing both the story and their sanity.

Hungary has a rich history of struggle and survival. The first Hungarians were fierce horseback warriors known as the Magyars who settled in the region. Later, Hungarians repeatedly found themselves between two major powers, such as seen in this book with the Habsburg and Ottoman Empires vying for control. This element of Hungarian history contributes significantly to the culture and will of its people.

I relied heavily on the work of Kimberly L. Craft, particularly the translated material from Báthory's trial and letters. I am grateful for Craft's dedication to using primary source material and her work in this little (for English speaking audiences) illuminated history.

ACKNOWLEDGMENTS

I wanted thank several people who were integral to the development of this book.

To my husband, Michael, for taking the time to read draft after draft. From day one you believed in me.

To Levente for the long and enlightening conversations about his home, culture and the Hungarian people. Thank you for not only taking the time to talk with me candidly, but also for your excitement over my interest and going so far as to translate your mother's recipes for me.

To Alice, Corwin, and Violet: Thank you greatly for your wise words and guidance in my efforts to write Anna correctly. Thank you so much for sharing yourselves with me, contributing to and reading this book for sensitivity.

To Nick for believing in this story and giving me a chance to share it with others.

I am humbled and thankful for you all.

ABOUT THE AUTHOR

K.P. Kulski's short fiction has appeared in Unnerving Magazine, as well as anthologies *Typhon Vol. 2*, and *Fierce Tales Shadow Realms*. Born in Hawaii to a Korean mother and American military father, she spent her youth wandering and living in many places both inside and outside the United States. She's a veteran of the U.S. Navy and Air Force and now teaches college history courses with a special interest in the experience of women in the classical and medieval worlds.

News and links to other publications can be found on her website - garnetonwinter.com.

WITHDRAWN